"I do not intend to play out my personal life in some gossip column," Richard said.

"What the hell were you thinking?"

"Me?" Melanie said, radiating indignation. "I had nothing to do with this. This isn't exactly great for my reputation, either."

"Who else knew you were down at my country home?" he demanded, then stared at her stricken face as understanding dawned. "Destiny, of course. She wants us together." If he hadn't known it before, he did now. This was the act of a very determined matchmaker.

"You mean me working for you," Melanie replied, still trying for a positive spin.

"No, *together* together," he said impatiently. "A couple."

"This is crazy," Melanie said. "Destiny can't just manipulate us into doing what she wants. We've decided that we're completely unsuited." She met his gaze. "Haven't we?"

Dear Reader,

Well, if it's true that March comes in like a lion and goes out like a lamb, you're going to need some fabulous romantic reads to get you through the remaining cold winter nights. Might we suggest starting with a new miniseries by bestselling author Sherryl Woods? In *Isn't It Rich?*, the first of three books in Ms. Wood's new MILLION DOLLAR DESTINIES series, we meet Richard Carlton, one of three brothers given untold wealth from his aunt Destiny. But in pushing him toward beautiful—if klutzy—PR executive Melanie Hart, Aunt Destiny provides him with riches that even money can't buy!

In *Bluegrass Baby* by Judy Duarte, the next installment in our MERLYN COUNTY MIDWIVES miniseries, a handsome but commitment-shy pediatrician shares a night of passion with a down-to-earth midwife. But what will he do when he learns there might be a baby on the way? Karen Rose Smith continues the LOGAN'S LEGACY miniseries with *Take a Chance on Me*, in which a sexy, single CEO finds the twin sister he never knew he had—and in the process is reunited with the only woman he ever loved. In *Where You Least Expect It* by Tori Carrington, a fugitive accused of a crime he didn't commit decides to put down roots and dare to dream of the love, life and family he thought he'd never have. Arlene James wraps up her miniseries THE RICHEST GALS IN TEXAS with *Tycoon Meets Texan!* in which a handsome billionaire who can have any woman he wants sets his sights on a beautiful Texas heiress. She clearly doesn't need his money, so *whatever* can she want with him? And when a police officer opens his door to a nine-months-pregnant stranger in the middle of a blizzard, he finds himself called on to provide both personal and professional services, in *Detective Daddy* by Jane Toombs.

So bundle up, and take heart—spring is coming! And so are six more sensational stories about love, life and family, coming next month from Silhouette Special Edition!

All the best,

Gail Chasan
Senior Editor

SHERRYL WOODS

ISN'T IT RICH?

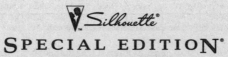

Silhouette®

SPECIAL EDITION®

Published by Silhouette Books

America's Publisher of Contemporary Romance

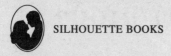

SILHOUETTE BOOKS

ISBN 0-373-24597-1

ISN'T IT RICH?

Copyright © 2004 by Sherryl Woods

This edition published by arrangement with Harlequin Books S.A.

® and TM are trademarks of Harlequin Books S.A., used under license.
Trademarks indicated with ® are registered in the United States Patent
and Trademark Office, the Canadian Trade Marks Office and in other
countries.

Visit Silhouette at www.eHarlequin.com

Printed in U.S.A.

Books by Sherryl Woods

SHERRYL WOODS

has written more than seventy-five novels. She also operates her own bookstore, Potomac Sunrise, in Colonial Beach, Virginia. If you can't visit Sherryl at her store, then be sure to drop her a note at P.O. Box 490326, Key Biscayne, FL 33149 or check out her Web site at www.sherrylwoods.com.

CAST OF CHARACTERS

Richard Carlton—A workaholic and born leader, he insists—and thrives—on a predictable, well-ordered life. As the oldest of three orphaned brothers and head of Carlton Industries, he takes responsibility for the company and his family seriously. Maybe a little too seriously.

Melanie Hart—She's already accomplished a lot in the tough world of marketing because she's a genius at seeing the big picture and planning a strategy for success. But details tend to elude her—as has romance. She's exactly the kind of woman to drive a man like Richard crazy, which is precisely why she's been handpicked to bring love into his life.

Destiny Carlton—Years ago, Richard's aunt sacrificed her madcap lifestyle in the south of France to come home and care for her orphaned nephews. As terrifying as she found the prospect, she's actually succeeded in getting them all to adulthood with a minimum of disasters. But until they're happily married, she won't consider her duty done—and her first matchmaking project is to get Richard to the altar.

One goal-oriented man, one slightly offbeat woman, and Destiny's touch… It's the perfect recipe for love!

Chapter One

Richard Carlton made three business calls on his cell phone, scowled impatiently at the antique clock on the wall of his favorite Old Town Alexandria seafood restaurant, made two more calls, then frowned at the Rolex watch on his wrist.

Five more minutes and he was history. He was only here as a favor to his Aunt Destiny. He'd promised to give some supposedly brilliant marketing whiz kid a chance at the consultant's contract for the family corporation's public relations campaign despite her lack of experience working with a major worldwide conglomerate.

He was also looking for a consultant who could help him launch his first political campaign. His intention had been to hire someone more seasoned than this woman Destiny was recommending, but his aunt was very persuasive when she put her mind to something.

"Just meet with her. Have a nice lunch. Give her a chance to sell *you* on her talent. After all," Aunt Destiny had said with a suspicious gleam in her eye, "nobody on earth is a tougher sell than you, right?"

Richard had given his aunt a wry look. "You flatter me."

She'd patted his cheek as if he were twelve again and she was trying to call attention gently to one of his flaws. "Not really, darling."

Destiny Carlton was the bane of his existence. He doubted if there was another aunt like her in the universe. When he was barely twelve, she'd breezed into his life twenty-four hours after his parents' small plane had crashed in the fog-shrouded Blue Ridge Mountains.

His father's older sister, Destiny had lived a nomad's life, cavorting with princes in European capitals, gambling in Monaco, skiing in Swiss Alpine resorts, then settling into a farmhouse in Provence where she'd begun painting more seriously, eventually selling her works in a small gallery on Paris's Left Bank. She was exotic and eccentric and more fun than anyone Richard or his younger brothers had ever met. She'd been just what three terrified little boys had needed.

A selfish woman would have scooped them up and taken them back to France, then resumed her own life, but not Destiny. She had plunged into unexpected motherhood with the same passionate enthusiasm and style with which she embraced life. She'd turned their previously well-ordered lives into a chaos of adventures in the process, but there had never been a doubt in their minds that she loved them. They, in turn, adored her, even when she was at her most maddening, as she had been lately, ever since she'd gotten some bee in her bonnet about the three of them needing to settle down. To her despair, he, Mack and Ben had been incredibly resistant to her urgings.

Over the years, despite Destiny's strong influence, Richard had clung tenaciously to the more somber lessons of his father. Work hard and succeed. Give back to the community. Be somebody. The adages had been drilled into him practically from infancy. Even at twelve, he'd felt the weight of responsibility for the generations-old Carlton Industries sitting squarely on his thin shoulders. Though an outsider had held the temporary reins upon his father's death, there was no question that the company would eventually be Richard's to run. A place would have been found for his brothers as well, if either of them had wanted it. But neither had shown the slightest interest, not back then and not now.

Back then, while his brothers had gone home after school to play their games, Richard had taken the family obligation to heart. Every weekday he'd gone to the historic old brick building that housed the corporate offices.

Destiny had tried her best to interest him in reading novels of all kinds, from the classics to science fiction and fantasy, but he'd preferred to scour the company books, studying the neatly aligned columns of figures that told the story of decades of profit and loss. The order and logic of it soothed him in a way he had been helpless to explain to her or to anyone. Even now, he had a better understanding of business than he did of people.

When he was twenty-three and had his M.B.A. from the prestigious Wharton School of Business, Richard slipped into the company presidency without raising so much as an eyebrow among the employees or among the worldwide CEOs with whom Carlton Industries did business. Most assumed he'd been all but running it behind the scenes since his father's death, anyway. Even as a kid, he'd displayed amazing confidence in his own decision-making.

Now, at thirty-two, he had the company on the track his father would have expected, expanding bit by bit with a strategic merger here, a hostile acquisition there. He was still young, successful and one of the city's most eligible bachelors. Unfortunately, his relationships tended to be brief once the women in his life realized they were always likely to take a back seat to the pressing—and often far more interesting—needs of the family company. The last woman he'd dated had told him he was a cold, dispassionate son of a bitch. He hadn't argued. In fact, he was pretty sure she had it just about right. Business never let him down. People did. He stuck to what he could trust.

Since he'd been so unsuccessful at romance, he'd turned his attention elsewhere in recent months. He'd been considering a run for office, perhaps the Alexandria City Council for starters. His father had expected all of his sons to climb to positions of power, not just in the corporate world, but in their community and the nation. Helping to shape Richard's image and get his name into print as a precursor to this was just part of what his new marketing consultant would be handling.

His timetable—okay, his father's oft-expressed timetable—for this was right on track, too. His father had espoused the need for short-term and long-term strategic planning. Richard had doubled the number of years his father had planned ahead for. He liked knowing where he should be—where he *would* be— ten, twenty, even thirty years down the road.

For someone whose precise schedule was so detailed, wasting precious minutes out of his jam-packed day waiting for a woman who was now twenty minutes late pretty much drove him crazy. Out of time and out of patience, Richard snapped his fingers. The maître d' appeared instantly.

"Yes, Mr. Carlton?"

"Could you put my coffee on my account, please, Donald? My guest hasn't arrived, and I have another appointment to get to back at my office."

"No charge for the coffee, sir. Would you like the chef to box up a salad?"

"No, thanks."

"Shall I get your coat, then?"

"Didn't wear one."

"Then at least let me call a taxi for you. It's started to snow quite heavily. The sidewalks and streets are treacherous. Perhaps that's why your guest is late."

Richard wasn't interested in finding excuses for the no-show, just in getting back to work. "If the weather's that bad, I can walk back sooner than you can get a taxi here. Thanks, anyway, Donald. And if Ms. Hart ever shows up, please tell her…" His voice trailed off. He decided the message he'd like to have relayed was better left unsaid. It was bound to come back to haunt him with his aunt, who was one of Donald's favorite customers. Though he considered his duty to Destiny's young friend done, his aunt might not see it the same way. "Just tell her I had to go."

"Yes, sir."

He opened the front door of the restaurant, stepped outside onto the slick sidewalk and ran straight into a battering ram. If he hadn't had a firm grip on the door, he'd have been on the ground. Instead, the woman who'd hit him headfirst in the midsection, stared up at him with huge, panicked brown eyes fringed with long, dark lashes just as her feet skidded out from under her.

Richard caught her inches from the icy ground and steadied her. Even though she was bundled up for the weather, she felt delicate. A faint frisson of something that felt like protectiveness hit him. It was something he'd previously experienced only with his younger brothers and his aunt. Most of the women in his life were so strong and capable, he'd never felt the least bit inclined to protect them from anything.

The woman closed her eyes, then opened them again and winced as she surveyed his face. "Please don't tell me you're Richard Carlton," she said, then sighed before he could respond. "But of course you are. You look exactly like the picture your aunt showed me.

"That's the way my day has gone," she rattled on. "First I get a cab driver who couldn't find his way to the corner without a map, then we get stuck behind a trash truck and then the snow starts coming down worse than a blizzard in the Rockies." She gazed at him hopefully, brushing at a stray strand of hair that was teasing at her still pink cheek. "I don't suppose you'd like to go back in, sit down and let me make a more dignified entrance?"

Richard bit back a sigh of his own. "Melanie Hart, I presume."

She gazed at him, her expression thoughtful. "I could pretend to be somebody else, and we could forget all about this unfortunate incident. I could call your office later, apologize profusely for missing you, make another appointment and start over in a very businesslike way."

"You're actually considering lying to me?"

"It would be a waste of time, wouldn't it?" she said with apparent regret. "I've already given myself away. I knew this whole lunch thing was a mistake. I make a much better impression in a conference room. I think it's the setting. People tend to take you more seriously if you can use an overhead projector and all sorts of charts and graphs. Anyway, I told Destiny that, but she insisted lunch would be better. She says you're less cranky on a full stomach."

"How lovely of her to share that," Richard said, vowing to have yet another wasted talk with his aunt about discussing him with anyone and everyone. If he did decide to run for office, her loose tongue would doom his chances before he got started.

"I don't suppose your stomach's full now?" Melanie Hart asked hopefully.

"No."

"Then you're bound to be cranky, so I'll just slip on inside and try to figure out how I managed to mess up the most important job interview of my entire life."

"If you decide you want an outside opinion, give me a call," Richard said.

He considered brushing right on past this walking disaster, but she looked so genuinely forlorn he couldn't seem to bring himself to do it. Besides, Destiny had said she was very good at what she did, and Destiny was seldom wrong about personnel matters. She was a good judge of people, at least when she didn't let emotion cloud her judgment. Richard very much feared this was one of those instances when her heart might have overruled her head. Still…

He tucked a hand under Melanie Hart's elbow and steered her inside. "Thirty minutes," he said tersely as Donald beamed at them and led them back to the table Richard had vacated just moments earlier. It had a fresh tablecloth, fresh place settings and a lit candle. He was almost certain that candle hadn't been there before. He had a suspicious feeling Donald had been expecting him back all along and had hoped a little atmosphere would improve his sour mood. No doubt the maître d' and his aunt were in cahoots. He'd probably called Destiny with a report five seconds after Richard had walked out.

When Donald had brought a fresh pot of coffee, Richard glanced at his watch. "Twenty-four minutes, Ms. Hart. Make 'em count."

Melanie reached for her attaché case and promptly knocked over her water glass…straight into his lap.

Richard leaped up as the icy water soaked through his pants. The day was just getting better and better.

"Oh, my God, I am so sorry," Melanie said, on her feet, napkin in hand, poised to sop up the water.

Richard considered letting her do it, just to see how she reacted once she realized exactly where she was touching him, but apparently she caught on to the problem. She handed the napkin to him.

"Sorry," she said again while he spent several minutes trying to dry himself off. "I swear to you that I am not normally such a klutz.'' At his doubtful look, she added, "Really, I'm not.''

"If you say so.''

"If you want to leave, I will totally understand. If you tell me never to darken your door, I'll understand that, too.'' Her chin came up and she looked straight into his eyes. "But you'll be making a terrible mistake.''

She was a bold one, no question about that. Richard paused in his futile attempt to dry his trousers. "How so?''

"I'm exactly what you need, Mr. Carlton. I know how to get attention.''

"Yes, I can see that,'' he said wryly. "There's unforgettable and then there's disastrous. I'm hoping for something a little more positive.''

"I can do that,'' she insisted. "I have the contacts. I'm clever and innovative. I know exactly how to sell my clients to the media. In fact, I have a preliminary plan right here for your campaign and for Carlton Industries.''

When she started to reach for her attaché case again, Richard grabbed the remaining water glass on the table and moved it a safe distance away, then sat back down while she scattered a flurry of papers in every direction. When she was finally done, he said, "I appreciate your enthusiasm, Ms. Hart, I really do, but this isn't going to work.'' To avoid hurting her feelings, he tried to temper his dismissal. "I need someone a little more seasoned.''

He refrained from adding that he wanted someone less ditzy, someone a little less inclined to remind him with every breath that she was a female and that he was a male who hadn't had sex for several months now. He did not need an employee who stirred up all these contradictory reactions in him. In this day and age that was a lawsuit waiting to happen.

His response to Melanie Hart bemused him. He'd gone from annoyance to anger to attraction in the space of—he glanced at his watch—less than twenty-five minutes. Relieved that her allotted time was nearly over, he tapped his Rolex. "Time's about up, Ms. Hart. Nice to meet you. I wish you luck and best success."

She gave him that forlorn, doe-eyed look that made his stomach clench and his pulse gallop erratically.

"You're kissing me off, aren't you?" she said.

It was an unfortunate turn of phrase. Richard suddenly couldn't stop looking at her mouth, which was soft and full and very, very kissable. He obviously needed to find the time to start dating again, if he was going to react this way to a woman as wildly inappropriate as Melanie Hart.

"I wouldn't put it that way," he said finally. "I'm just saying it's a bad match. If you're as talented as my aunt says, you'll be snapped up by another company in no time at all."

"I already have other clients, Mr. Carlton. In fact, my business is thriving," she said stiffly. "I wanted to work for you and for Carlton Industries because I think I have something to offer you that your in-house staff cannot."

"Which is?"

"A fresh perspective that would drag your corporate and personal image out of the Dark Ages." She stood up. "Perhaps I was wrong. Perhaps your current stuffy image has it exactly right."

As Richard stared, she whirled around and marched

out of the restaurant with her head held high, her back straight and the tiniest, most provocative sway of her narrow hips he'd seen in a long time.

Damn, what was happening to him? The infernal woman had just mowed him down, soaked him with water and told him off, and he still couldn't take his eyes off of her. Of course, the real problem was that she wanted to work for him...and for some totally insane and inexplicable reason, he wanted her in his bed.

"And then I soaked him with water," Melanie related to Destiny Carlton a few hours later over drinks at what had once been the Carlton family home. Now Destiny apparently lived there alone. "I'll be lucky if he doesn't catch pneumonia and sue me. I think I can pretty much count on getting a polite rejection letter in tomorrow's mail just to take away any lingering doubts I might have that he absolutely, positively hated me. Heck, he'll probably send it over by courier tonight to make sure I don't come waltzing into his office tomorrow and burn the building down."

Destiny laughed, oddly delighted by this report. "Oh, darling, it couldn't have gone better. Richard is much too pompous. He takes himself too seriously. You're just the breath of fresh air he needs."

"I really don't think he saw the humor in the situation," Melanie said with genuine regret.

She'd liked Richard. Okay, he was a little bit rigid and standoffish, but she could improve on that. She could coach him on smiling more frequently. She'd had one glimpse of his killer smile and it had made her knees weak. If he smiled more and frowned less, he could win over every female voter in Alexandria, no matter where he stood on the issues. She really thought she could do great things for Carlton Industries and for its CEO. It was a challenge she'd been looking forward to. Now she'd never have the chance. And while her company wasn't exactly thriving, the way she'd told him it was, a coup like this would have assured its future.

"I'll talk to him. I'm sure I can smooth things over," Destiny said.

"Please, no," Melanie insisted. "You've done enough. You got me the interview in the first place. I'm the one who blew it. Maybe I can think of some way to salvage things."

"I'm sure you can," Destiny said with an encouraging smile. "You're very clever at such things. I knew that the moment we met."

"We met when I dented your rear fender," Melanie reminded her.

"But it only took a few minutes for you to convince me it was time for a new car, anyway. You had me on the dealer's lot and behind the wheel of my snappy little red convertible within the hour, and I'm no pushover," Destiny asserted.

Melanie laughed. "Who are you kidding? You were dying to buy a new car. I just gave you a reason and steered you to a client I knew would give you a great deal."

"But don't you see? That's exactly what marketing is all about—convincing people to go ahead and get something they've wanted but haven't thought they needed. Now you merely have to convince my nephew that he—or, rather, Carlton Industries—can't live without you."

An alarm suddenly went off in Melanie's head at

Destiny's slip of the tongue. She studied the older woman warily, but there was nothing in her friend's eyes to suggest duplicity. Still, she had to ask. "Destiny, you're not matchmaking, are you?"

"Me? Matchmaking for Richard? Heavens no. I wouldn't waste the energy. He would never take my advice when it comes to matters of the heart."

She made the protest sound very convincing, but Melanie didn't quite buy it. Destiny Carlton was a kind, smart, fascinating woman, but she clearly had a sneaky streak. She also adored her nephews. Melanie had picked up on that the first time they'd met. Destiny had gone on and on about their attributes and how she despaired of ever seeing them settle down. Who knew what she might do to get them married off?

"I'm not in the market for a husband," Melanie told her firmly. "You know that, don't you?"

"But you are in the market for a challenging job, right? That hasn't changed?"

"No, that hasn't changed."

"Well, then," Destiny said cheerily. "Let's put our heads together and come up with a plan. Nobody knows Richard's weak spots better than I do."

"He has weaknesses?" Melanie asked skeptically. He'd struck her as tough, competent and more than a little arrogant. If there was a chink in his armor, she hadn't spotted it, and she was well trained to spot flaws that the media might exploit and see that they were corrected or hidden from view.

Destiny beamed at her. "He's a man, isn't he? All men can be won over if the tactics are right. Have I told you about the duke?"

"The one who chased you all over Europe?"

"No, dear, that was a prince. This man—the duke—was the love of my life," she confided, her expression nostalgic. Then she shook her head. "Well, that's in the past. Best not to go there. Let's concentrate on Richard. There's a little cottage on the river about eighty miles from here. It's very peaceful. I think I can get him down there this weekend."

Melanie eyed her friend warily. She wasn't sure she liked the sound of this. The last time she'd trusted Destiny's instincts over her own, look what had happened.

"And?" she asked cautiously.

"Then you show up with some of his favorite gourmet food—I'll help you plan the menu—and your marketing plan. He won't be able to resist."

There were so many things wrong with that scheme, Melanie didn't know where to begin. If doing a presentation in a restaurant was awkward and unprofessional, then chasing the man to some out-of-the-way cottage was downright ludicrous and rife with the potential for disaster.

"If he goes there to relax, won't he be furious if I intrude?" she asked, trying to curb Destiny's enthusiasm for the idea.

Destiny waved off her concern. "He doesn't go there to relax. He goes there to get more work done. He says it's less noisy than his place here."

"Then I'll still be an unwelcome interruption," Melanie protested.

"Not if we get the menu exactly right," Destiny said. "The way to a man's heart, et cetera. I have a few bottles of his favorite wine right here. You can take those along, too."

Melanie wasn't convinced. "It seems a little risky.

No, it seems a *lot* risky. I am not one of his favorite people right now.''

Her comment fell on deaf ears. ''Anything worth having is worth a little risk,'' Destiny said blithely. ''What can he do? Slam the door in your face? I've raised him better than that.''

That didn't sound so awful. Melanie weighed the prospect of facing Richard's annoyance once again against the possibility of getting a dream contract for her new company. Landing Carlton Industries would be a coup. Helping to shape Richard Carlton's first run for political office would be an even bigger one, especially if he won. In this politics-happy region where candidates from every state in the country abounded, she'd soon be able to name her own price.

Making her decision, she gave Destiny a weak smile. ''Okay, then. What am I serving?''

Chapter Two

Three large hampers of food arrived at Melanie's small home in Alexandria's Delray neighborhood not far from historic Old Town at two o'clock on Friday, along with a heavy vellum envelope addressed in Destiny's elaborate script. Melanie regarded it all with grim resignation. This was really going to happen. She was really going to invade Richard Carlton's privacy and try to convince him that he needed her—professionally, at any rate.

As soon as the uniformed chauffeur bowed and left, Melanie's assistant and best friend slipped out of the office that had been created from what was meant to be the master bedroom in the 1940s-era house, peeked into the wicker baskets crowding the foyer, then turned to her.

"Wow, Mel, is someone trying to seduce you?" Becky asked, clearly intrigued by the excess.

"Hardly," Melanie said. "In fact, I'm pretty sure the hope is that I'll seduce Richard Carlton."

Becky gave her a hard, disbelieving look. "I thought that meeting went really, really badly."

"It did. But his aunt seems to think I can salvage it, if I just ply him with food and alcohol in a secluded little cottage by the sea."

Becky, who had solid business instincts under her romantic facade, didn't seem impressed by the theory. "And how exactly are you supposed to coax him into going there with you?"

"Destiny is taking care of that." Melanie slit open the envelope, read the message, glanced at the two sheets of typed instructions included, then sighed.

"What's that?" Becky asked, eyeing the papers with suspicion.

"My marching orders," Melanie said wryly. "She even thought to include cooking instructions. She must know about my tendency to burn water."

Becky chuckled, caught Melanie's sour look and immediately sobered. "Since you've apparently bought into this idiotic scheme, then I think it was very thoughtful of her."

"I'm sure she was just thinking of her nephew's health."

"Tell me again why she's so determined to help you land this contract," Becky prompted.

"I wish I could say that I'd impressed the hell out of her with my professional credentials, but that's not it. She thinks Richard is stuffy and I'm a breath of fresh air," Melanie explained. At least that had been the reason Destiny had expressed for going to all this trouble.

"In other words, she has an ulterior motive,"

Becky concluded, leaping to her own conclusion. "The whole seduction thing."

"Don't say that," Melanie pleaded, not liking that Becky had almost instantly confirmed her own suspicions. "Don't even think it. This is business, not personal."

"Yeah, right."

"It is, at least for me. If I get this contract, I will no longer have to lie awake nights worrying about whether I can pay your salary."

"Then by all means, get down to this cottage and start cooking," Becky said, snapping the lids on the hampers closed. "By the way, if that pie doesn't win him over, then the man's not human. It smells heavenly. I had a candle once that smelled exactly like that, like warm cherry pie just out of the oven. Every time I lit it, I ate. I gained ten pounds before the darn thing finally burned out."

Melanie chuckled. From the day they'd met in college, Becky had claimed that everything up to and including high humidity caused her to gain weight. She was constantly bemoaning the ten pounds she supposedly needed to lose. The extra weight hadn't hurt her social life. She had the kind of lush curves that caused men to fall all over themselves whenever she walked into a room.

"Come on, Mel, have a heart and get this stuff out of here," she begged now. "I'll hold down the fort for the rest of the day."

Melanie knew she couldn't very well back out now. She'd agreed to this crazy scheme. She had to follow through with it, and she might as well get on the road and get it over with. Reluctantly she gathered up her coat, her purse and her business plan for Carlton Industries.

"You're going to have to help me haul this food out to the car," she said. "I think Destiny went a little overboard and packed enough for the weekend, not just dinner."

"Maybe she has high hopes for just how well dinner is going to go," Becky suggested, struggling to balance two heavy wicker baskets as she followed Melanie to her car.

"Or maybe she's counting on a blizzard," Melanie replied grimly. It would be just her luck to get herself snowed in with a man who'd all but said he never wanted to lay eyes on her again. "Have you seen a weather report?"

"Haven't needed to," Becky said, gesturing toward the western sky, which was a dull gray, the usual precursor to snow.

Melanie groaned. "Okay, then, if it does snow and I'm not back on Monday, promise me you'll come and dig me out. Buy a damn snowplow if you have to."

"Maybe I'll just wait to hear you confirm that on Monday," Becky said with a sly grin. "Could be you won't want to be rescued."

"Promise me," Melanie said, gritting her teeth. "Or I swear I will fire you, even if I get this contract and we're rolling in money."

"Fine. Fine," Becky soothed, still fighting a grin. "I'll come rescue you if you're not back by Monday." The smile broke free. "Or at least I'll tell the cops where to start looking for the body."

Melanie winced. "Don't joke about that. It could go that badly."

Becky's expression sobered at once. "Mel, you're really worried about this, are you?"

"Not that he'll kill me, no," Melanie said honestly. "But it's entirely likely that he'll toss me right back out into the snow and I'll die of humiliation."

"Nobody dies of humiliation, at least not in the public relations business. We're the masters of spin. Remember that. It's what we do best."

"I'm sure knowing that will warm me right up when I'm sitting in a snowbank freezing my butt off," Melanie said.

Becky laughed. "Just keep your cell phone handy so you can call nine-one-one. I hear the paramedics really get off on trying to save people from frostbite in that particular region."

So much for sympathy and support from the woman who was not only her assistant but her closest friend. Melanie started her car and skidded down her icy driveway till she hit the cleared pavement of the road. She did not look back, because she was pretty certain that traitorous Becky was probably laughing her head off.

Richard wasn't at all sure how he'd let his aunt convince him to spend the weekend at the cottage, especially since he'd been down here for a couple of hours and there was still no sign of Destiny. Nor had she phoned. He was beginning to worry. Not that a woman who'd traipsed all over the globe on her own couldn't handle anything that came up, but she was his aunt. Ever since his parents had died, he'd worried obsessively about everyone who was left in his life. He'd barely been able to watch Mack play professional football because a part of him had been terrified that his younger brother would have his neck snapped by some overly aggressive defensive player. As it turned out, it had been a far less deadly knee injury that had ended Mack's career on the field. Richard had been the only one in the family relieved to have Mack safely ensconced in the team's administrative office as a part owner these days.

When Richard finally heard footsteps on the front porch, he threw open the door. "It's about time," he groused to cover his irrational concern. Then he got a good look at the bundled-up woman outside. "You!"

"Hello again," Melanie said cheerfully. "Surprise!"

Richard felt his stomach ricochet wildly, and not in a good way. "What was Destiny thinking?" he murmured, half to himself. She was behind this. She had to be.

As for Melanie, she was obviously a lot tougher than he'd realized. The blasted woman didn't seem to be the least bit put off by his lack of welcome. She beamed and brushed right past him into the small foyer, peering around at the living room with undisguised curiosity.

"I'm fairly sure Destiny's only thought was that you'd probably be starving by now," she said, giving a totally unnecessary reply to his rhetorical question. "She asked me to tell you she was sorry about the change in plans. Something came up."

"Yeah, I'll bet," he muttered. Then the scent of warm cherry pie wafted toward him. "What's in the basket?"

"Give me a few minutes to unpack it all and I'll

show you. By the way, there are two more baskets in the car. If you'll get those, I'll deal with this one.''

"You could just make your delivery and head back to Alexandria," Richard said, still holding out hope that he could cut this encounter short.

"On an empty stomach? I don't think so. I've spent the last two hours smelling this cherry pie—I'm not leaving till I've had some. There are a couple of steaks in one of the baskets and potatoes for baking, butter *and* sour cream—which is a little excessive, if you ask me—plus a huge Caesar salad. There are also a couple of excellent bottles of French wine. I'm told it's your favorite, though personally I think the California cabernets are just as good and far less expensive.''

Destiny at her sneakiest, Richard concluded with a sigh. She'd sent all of his favorite foods, despite her alleged concern about his cholesterol. He picked up the basket and closed the door, then stepped aside to permit Melanie to come all the way into the cottage. "Come on in.''

"Said the spider to the fly," Melanie said, injecting an ominous note into her voice as she brushed right past him and headed with unerring accuracy right toward the kitchen. Destiny had probably given her a complete floor plan. He couldn't help wondering if his aunt had also provided a key, in case he tried to lock her protégé out.

He gave Melanie a wry look. "Where we're concerned, I think you've got that backward. I'm the intended victim here.''

"Whatever," she said, clearly unconcerned. She met his gaze, her eyes a dark, liquid brown. "Those other baskets," she prodded.

"What?" Richard blinked, then grasped her meaning. "Oh, sure. I'll get 'em now." He fled the kitchen and the disconcerting woman who seemed to be taking it over. Maybe a blast of frigid air would clear his head and help him to come up with some way to get her out of there.

Unfortunately, by the time he started back inside, nothing short of hauling Melanie bodily back to her car and turning on the engine had come to him. Since that was pretty much out of the question, he was doomed. A big fat snowflake splatted on his forehead as if to confirm his decision. He looked up, and several more snowflakes hit him in the face.

"Great, just great," he muttered. The minute—no, the second—he spotted Destiny again, he was going to wring her neck.

Inside he plunked the baskets down on the round oak table where he, Destiny and his brothers had shared many a meal and played many a game of Monopoly or gin rummy. He grabbed the slim local phone book from the counter and began almost desperately leafing through the pages. There was an inn nearby. If Melanie left now, right this instant, she could be snuggled up in front of *its* fire in minutes.

"Who are you calling?" she asked as she unpacked the food.

"The inn."

"Why?"

"It's snowing. You're going to need a place to stay."

Her determinedly cheerful expression finally faded. "It's snowing," she echoed.

"Hard," he added grimly.

She sighed and sank down at the table. "Do you

think it's possible that your aunt controls the weather, too?''

She asked it so plaintively that Richard couldn't help the chuckle that sneaked up the back of his throat. ''I've wondered that myself at times,'' he admitted. ''She has a lot of powers, but I'm fairly certain that's not one of them.''

He gave his guest an encouraging look. ''It'll be okay. The inn is lovely. It's not a bad place to be stranded.''

As he spoke, he dialed the number. It rang and rang, before an answering machine finally came on and announced that the inn was closed until after the first of the year. He heard the message with a sinking heart. There was a small motel nearby, but it was no place he'd send his worst enemy, much less Melanie Hart, not if he ever expected to look his aunt in the face again. Of course, he planned to strangle her, so her opinion was likely to be short-lived.

''What?'' Melanie asked as he slowly hung up.

''The inn's closed till after January first.''

She stood up at once and reached for her coat. ''Then I'll leave now. I'm sure I can get back up to town before the roads get too bad.''

''And have me worrying for hours about whether you've skidded into a ditch? I don't think so,'' he said, reaching the only decision he could live with. ''You'll stay here. There are lots of rooms.''

''I don't want to be an inconvenience,'' she told him. ''There are bound to be some other places I can get a room, if the roads get too bad once I start back.''

''No,'' he said flatly, carefully avoiding her gaze so she wouldn't see just how disturbed he was by the prospect of being stranded here with her for an hour, much less a day or two.

"I feel awful about this," she said with what sounded like genuine regret. "I knew it was a bad idea, but you know how your aunt is. She gets something into her head, and everyone else just gets swept along."

"Tell me about it."

"As soon as we eat, I'll go to my room and you won't have to spend another second worrying about me," she assured him. "I'll be quiet as a mouse. You won't even know I'm here."

"Wouldn't that pretty much defeat the purpose of this visit?" he asked.

"Purpose?"

"To talk me into reconsidering hiring you," he said. "We both know Destiny didn't send you down here just to deliver dinner. Her driver could have done that."

"Caught," Melanie conceded, looking only marginally chagrined.

"Well, then, now's your chance. Start talking," he told her as he opened a bottle of wine to let it breathe.

"Not till we've eaten," she insisted. "I want every advantage I can get." She looked over the ingredients for their dinner, now spread out on the table. "Of course, if you want dinner to be edible, you might want to pitch in."

"You can't cook?"

"Let's just say that a peanut butter and jelly sandwich and microwaved oatmeal are my specialties."

Richard shook his head. "Move over," he said, nudging her aside with his hip, then almost immediately regretting the slight contact with her soft curves.

"And stay out of my way," he added for good measure.

She didn't seem to take offense. In fact, she looked downright relieved. "Can I set the table? Pour the wine?"

"Sure," he agreed. "The dishes and wineglasses are in the cabinet right up there."

He glanced over as she reached for them and found himself staring at an inch of pale skin as her sweater rode up from the waistband of her slacks. She had a very trim waist. He wanted very badly to skim a finger across that tiny bit of exposed flesh to see if it was as soft and satiny as it looked. He wasn't used to being turned on by so little. She had to be some kind of wizard to make him want her without half-trying. Only because he didn't want to let on how hot and bothered he was did he resist the desire to snag the bottom of her sweater and tug it securely back into place. He could just imagine her reaction to that. She'd know right then and there that she had the upper hand. Who knew how she'd use that little piece of information.

"Have you had this place a long time?" she asked when she finally had all the dishes in her arms. As she turned and set the precariously balanced load on the table, her sweater slid back into place, thank God.

"Since we were kids," he told her as he scrubbed the potatoes. "Destiny missed the water and the country when she came back from living in France, so we piled into the car one weekend and went exploring. She spotted this house and fell in love with it."

"I can understand why. The view of the Potomac is incredible. It must be wonderful to sit on the front porch in the summer and watch the boats on the water and listen to the waves.''

''I suppose it is,'' he said, distracted by the dreamy note in her voice.

Melanie gave him a knowing look. ''How long has it been since you've done that?''

''Years,'' he admitted. ''Usually when I come down here, I bring a pile of paperwork and never set foot outside. I come because it's peaceful and quiet and I know no one will interrupt me.'' He regarded her with a wry expression. ''Not usually, anyway.''

Melanie nodded as if she'd expected the response. ''I'd read that you were a workaholic.''

''Just proves the media gets it right once in a while.''

''Haven't you ever heard that all work and no play makes one dull?''

He shrugged. ''I never really cared.''

She studied him curiously. ''What kind of image do you see yourself projecting as a candidate?''

Richard paused as he was about to put the potatoes into the oven. He hadn't yet given the matter much thought. He should have. Instead, he'd based his decision to run for office on the expected progression of his life carefully planned out by his father, probably while Richard was still in diapers.

''I want people to know I'm honest,'' he began, considering his reply thoughtfully. ''I want them to believe that I'll work hard and that I'll care about their problems, about the issues that matter to them.''

''That's good,'' she said. ''But did you go to public school?''

''No.''

"Have you ever had to struggle for money, been out of work?"

"No."

"Ever been denied a place to live because of the color of your skin?"

He flushed slightly. "No."

"Do you have good medical insurance?"

"Of course. So do my employees."

"Ever had to go without a prescription because you couldn't afford it?"

"No." He saw where she was going, and it grated on his nerves.

"Then what makes you think they'll believe you can relate to their problems?" she asked.

"Look, I can't help that I've led a life of privilege, but I can care about people who haven't. I can be innovative about ways to solve their problems. I know a lot about business. Some of those principles can be applied to government as well," he said, barely able to disguise his irritation. "Look, I don't get this. If you think I'm such a lousy candidate, why do you want to work for me?"

She grinned. "So I can show you how to be a *good* candidate, maybe even a great one."

He shook his head at her audacity. "Confident, aren't you?"

"No more so than you are. You believe in *your*self. I believe in *my*self. That could be the beginning of a great team."

"Or a disaster waiting to happen," he said, not convinced. "Two egos butting heads at every turn."

"Maybe, but if we remember that we both have the same goal, I'm pretty sure that will get us through any rough patches."

Richard considered her theory as he heated the fancy grill that was part of the restaurant-caliber stove he'd had installed once he'd taken up gourmet cooking to relax. He tossed on the steaks. "How do you want it?" he asked.

Melanie stared at him, looking puzzled. "Want what?"

He grinned. "Your steak."

"Well-done," she said at once.

"I should have guessed."

"I suppose you eat yours raw," she muttered.

"Rare," he corrected.

"Same thing. It's all very macho."

"I suppose you think I should give up beef or something to appease the vegetarian voters."

"Don't be ridiculous. There must be a zillion very popular steak houses in the Washington area. There's your constituency."

"I like to think I can relate to people who prefer lobster, too."

She laughed and shook her head. "My work is so cut out for me."

"You don't have the job," he reminded her.

She stepped up beside him and snagged a slice of red pepper from the pan of vegetables he was sautéing. Then she grinned. "I will," she said with total confidence.

Richard got that same odd sensation in the pit of his stomach, the one he used to get right before a roller coaster crested the top of the tracks and pitched down in a mad burst of speed. He looked at Melanie as she licked a trace of olive oil from the tip of her finger and felt that same mix of excitement and fear.

He hadn't been in waters this deep and dangerous in years. Maybe never.

Damn Destiny. She'd known exactly what she was doing by pushing this woman into his life, and it didn't have a bloody thing to do with getting him elected to office or polishing the image of Carlton Industries around the globe. Melanie was to be the key player in Destiny's latest skirmish to marry him off.

Well, he didn't have to take the bait. He could keep his hormones under control and his hands to himself. No problem. At least, as long as Melanie stopped looking at him with those big, vulnerable brown eyes. Those eyes made him want to give her whatever she wanted, made him want to take whatever he wanted.

Yep, those eyes were trouble. Too bad she wasn't one of those sophisticated women who wore sunglasses night and day as part of their fashion statement. Then he might have a shot at sticking to his resolve.

As it was, he was probably doomed.

Chapter Three

Though he'd stopped scowling after his second glass of wine, Richard didn't seem as if he was being won over, Melanie concluded reluctantly. He was being civil, not friendly. And he definitely wasn't leaving her much of an opening to start pitching her PR plan. Drastic measures were called for. Destiny had seemed certain that food was the answer, so Melanie had added a touch of her own to the meal.

"I stopped and picked up ice cream for the pie," she told him, hoping she'd guessed right that a man who loved cherry pie would prefer it à la mode.

He actually smiled for the first time—a totally unguarded reaction, for once. Just as Melanie had remembered, the effect was devastating. The smile made his blue eyes sparkle and emphasized that there really were laugh lines at the corners. It also eased the tension in his square jaw.

"Acting against Destiny's warnings, no doubt," he said. "She probably has the cardiologist on standby as it is."

Melanie grinned back at him. "I have his name and number in my purse," she joked, then added more truthfully, "along with cooking instructions and directions to this place. Destiny left very little to chance."

He seemed uncertain whether to take her seriously. "Not that I would put it past her, but she didn't actually give you the name of a doctor, did she?"

Melanie laughed. "Okay, no, but she does seem to be concerned that your particular nutritional habits combined with your workaholic tendencies will land you in an early grave. Do you ever relax?"

"Sure," he said at once. "I'm here, aren't I?"

Melanie gestured toward the computer that he'd been glancing at longingly ever since her arrival. "Unless you're on there doing your Christmas shopping, I don't think this qualifies."

He regarded her with a vaguely puzzled expression. "When is Christmas?"

"Less than three weeks."

He nodded, then reached for the pocket computer he'd tossed on the counter earlier, and made a note.

"Reminding your secretary to get your shopping done?" she asked him.

He looked only slightly chagrined at having been caught. "Winifred's better at it than I am," he said, not sounding the least bit defensive. "She has more time, too. I give her a few extra hours off to do *her* shopping, along with mine."

Melanie nodded. "A successful man always knows how to delegate. Do you give her a budget? Suggestions? Does she tell you what's in the packages, so you're not as surprised as the recipients on Christmas morning? I've always wondered how that worked.''

He took the question seriously. ''Most of the time she puts little sticky labels on the wrapped boxes so I can add my own gift card. She seems to think my handwriting ought to be on there.'' His eyes glinted with sudden amusement. ''Occasionally, though, she likes to go for the shock value, especially with my brothers. Last year I gave my brother Mack—''

''The former Washington football hero,'' Melanie recalled.

''Exactly, and one of the city's most sought after bachelors.'' He grinned. ''My secretary bought him a rather large, shapely, inflatable female. I'm pretty sure Destiny had a hand in that one. She'd been trying to convince Mack that he doesn't have to make it his personal mission to date every woman in the entire Washington metropolitan area. She seemed to think he might be better able to commit to a woman with no expectations.''

''Your family has a very odd sense of humor, if you don't mind me saying so.''

''You don't know the half of it.''

''Did it work?''

''Not so's I've noticed,'' he admitted. ''Mack is still happily playing the field.''

''I see. And my job would be to see to it that no one else discovers these little family quirks?'' Melanie asked, daring to broach the subject that had brought her to this cozy, out-of-the-way cottage. ''If I get the job, that is.''

''I thought we'd pretty much settled that question last time we met,'' Richard said.

Melanie shook her head. "I didn't like the outcome. I'm here to change it."

"Darn. I thought maybe you were here to seduce me," he said, almost making his expressed disappointment sound sincere.

Melanie gave him a hard look. That was a line of conversation that needed to be cut short in a hurry. She hadn't liked the seduction angle when she'd guessed it was part of Destiny's plan. She liked it even less coming from Richard. Okay, maybe she was marginally intrigued, but it was a bad idea any way she looked at it.

"Not in a million years," she said emphatically.

He seemed startled by her vehemence. "Why is that?"

"Been there, done that."

His gaze narrowed. "Meaning?"

She opted for total honesty so he'd understand just how opposed she was. "I made the serious mistake of sleeping with my last boss. I thought I was madly in love with him and vice versa. When the affair ended, so did my job. Now I work for myself. I won't make the same mistake a second time, not with a boss, not with a client."

"Good rule of thumb," he agreed. "But I'm not your boss *or* your client."

"I want this consulting contract more than I want you," she declared, proud of herself for managing to make the claim without even a hint of a quaver in her voice. Deep down inside, she knew the balance of that equation could change if she let it.

He chuckled. "At least you're admitting to the attraction."

Melanie silently cursed the slip. "Doesn't matter,"

she insisted. "It's not powerful enough to make me lose my focus."

"Now there's the way to win a man's heart."

Realizing that her attempt to make a point might have bruised his ego, she quickly added, "Not that you're not attractive and rich and an incredible catch for some woman."

"Nice save."

"I'm quick on my feet in tense situations. It'll serve me well as I'm fending off the media when you decide to run for office."

"I thought the whole idea was to captivate the media, not to fend them off."

"Well, of course it is," she said irritably. The man had a way of twisting her words to suit himself. She leveled a look into his eyes to prove she could hold her own, no matter what the level of intimidation. "But there are bound to be things you don't want to talk about, skeletons in the closet, that sort of thing."

His expression turned grim. "I don't have skeletons in my closet."

"No trail of brokenhearted women who'll feel the need to tell all when the stakes are high?"

"No," he said tersely.

She studied him with a narrowed gaze. "Men?"

He laughed. "Hardly, unless you consider the accountant I fired for trying to steal from the company to be a potential problem."

"Good to know. Then you should be a dream client."

His gaze met hers and he shook his head. "I don't think so, Melanie."

"But I have a plan," she said, reaching for her

proposal. It was a darned good one, too. She'd slaved over it for days.

His gaze never left her face. "So do I."

Her pulse kicked up a notch. "We're not on the same track, are we?"

"Not so far," he agreed, his expression sober, his eyes filled with unexpected heat.

To Melanie's sincere regret, somewhere deep inside, she wasn't nearly as upset by that as she should have been. Even so, she was holding out for what *she* wanted...the very lucrative contract. Sleeping with Richard to get it simply wasn't in the cards.

"Then I suppose I should help you clean up," she said as if the rest of it didn't matter. "Then I'll get out of your hair so you can go back to work. Good thing I'm never without a good book to read."

"No room for negotiation?" he inquired.

"None," she said flatly.

"Fine," he said, giving up what had been little more than a fainthearted battle to begin with. "Never mind cleaning up. I'll take care of it. You can take the guest room at the top of the stairs on the left. The bathroom's next door."

It rankled that he thought he could dismiss her so easily. "You cooked," she said with determination. "I'll clean up."

She met his gaze, challenging him to argue. He didn't. He merely shrugged. "Suit yourself." He turned his back and headed to his computer. Within seconds, he appeared to be thoroughly engrossed in a screen of what appeared to her to be incomprehensible columns of figures.

Obviously the man didn't like to lose, didn't like the fact that she'd thwarted his plan to turn this week-

end into a romantic encounter. Never mind that the
encounter was one he hadn't really wanted. He was
obviously more than willing to take advantage of the
circumstances since the opportunity had presented it-
self. Of course, he was just as willing to forget about
it, which meant he'd only been toying with her, playing a game he'd been prepared to lose.

Ignoring Richard, Melanie managed to get the
dishes, pots and pans into the dishwasher with a minimum of banging, despite her desire to make as much
racket as possible. She still held out a slim hope that
in the clear light of day, Richard would recognize that
he had behaved badly and would at least consider her
proposal on its merits. Destiny believed her nephew
was a man of integrity, and Melanie very much
wanted to believe her friend was right.

"Good night," she muttered as she stalked past
him on her way upstairs.

He mumbled a response, as if he were totally distracted, but she knew better. She could feel his gaze
following her as she left the room and climbed the
stairs.

Inside the guest room, which had charming chintz
wallpaper above old-fashioned white beadboard especially suited to a beach cottage, Melanie sank onto
the queen-size bed with its antique iron headboard
and tried to figure out how the evening had gone so
dreadfully awry. It wasn't as if she'd never been prop-
ositioned before. It happened all the time. It wasn't
as if Richard had pushed after she'd said no. In fact,
he'd taken her at her word and remained reasonably
good-humored about the firm rejection.

And wasn't that the real problem? Had she wanted
him to ride roughshod over her objections? Had she

wanted him to sweep her into his arms, kiss her until she melted and then carry her up to this very romantic bed? She'd never been one to lie to herself, and the truth was that a part of her had wanted exactly that. Thankfully, sanity had prevailed—his apparently more so than hers. Her principles remained intact, as much a credit to his restraint as to her stern words. She would be able to face him in the morning with head held high.

She picked up a down pillow and pummeled it. Fat lot of comfort those principles were going to be during the rest of this long, cold night.

Richard was up at dawn after a restless night. He felt oddly disgruntled, as if he'd done something wrong, something he ought to apologize for, but damned if he knew what that was. He'd made his desire for Melanie clear. She'd said no. He'd accepted that. The exchange should have ended the evening with no hard feelings.

Instead, she'd stalked off as if he'd offended her. Damned if he would ever understand women. He thought he'd given her what she wanted, a night alone in her own bed.

Of course, what she really wanted was that consulting job, and he wasn't prepared to offer her that. She'd drive him crazy in days, maybe even hours.

He was drinking his first cup of his special-blend coffee, when he heard her tentative footsteps coming downstairs. Uncertain what to expect, he tightened his grip on his cup and watched the doorway with a grim expression.

Instead of the dour, accusing woman he was expecting, in walked Little Mary Sunshine, all smiles and bright eyes.

"Good morning," she said cheerfully. "Isn't the snow gorgeous? I've never been at the beach after a snowstorm before. It really is like a winter wonderland out there, don't you think?"

"I suppose," he said cautiously.

"Haven't you even looked outside?"

"Of course I have." The truth was, he'd been too dismayed by the sight of the impassable roads to take much joy in the picturesque landscape.

As if she'd read his mind, she laughed. "You're panicked because there's no chance of me getting out of here this morning, aren't you?"

"I'm sure you have things you'd rather be doing," he said defensively. "Places you'd rather be."

"Not really," she said cheerfully.

Richard stared at her. Only after he'd studied her closely did he detect the faint wariness in her eyes. She was putting on a show for him, and it was a pretty decent one. It had almost had him fooled.

"Want some breakfast?" he asked.

"Cereal will do."

"I was thinking of making French toast with maple syrup. That's what Destiny always makes when we're here. She considered it a vacation treat."

Her eyes lit up, and this time her enthusiasm seemed genuine. "And you can make French toast?"

He laughed at the hint of amazement in her voice. "It's not that hard."

He moved past her, gathered a few eggs, butter and milk from the refrigerator.

"I'll set the table," she said, heading toward the dishwasher.

"I've already put the dishes away," he told her.

"How long have you been up?"

"Hours."

She gave him a knowing look. "Couldn't sleep?"

"I'm always an early riser."

"Not me. I like sleeping in. Being up at dawn is unnatural."

"Not once you've seen a sunrise over the river," he said. "Grab a couple of plates and a bowl, then come over here."

She set the dishes on the table, then regarded him warily. "Why over there?"

"I'm going to teach you how to make this. You might as well go away from this weekend with one new skill."

She backed off as if he'd suggested teaching her alligator-wrestling. "I don't think so. You probably only have a dozen eggs here. I can ruin more than that without half-trying."

Richard refused to back down. "Over here, or I'll think you're scared of being close to me." He met her gaze. "Maybe even tempted to take me up on that proposition I made last night."

"That was a bad idea," she reminded him.

"Yeah, I got that."

"But I'm not scared of you."

He bit back a grin. "If you say so." He held out an egg. "Break this into the bowl. Try not to get any shell in there."

She smashed it with so much enthusiasm, he suspected she was pretending it was his skull. Egg and shell dribbled into the bowl. He dumped the mess into the sink and handed her another egg. "Try again."

"Wouldn't it be easier if you just went ahead and did it?"

"Easier, but you wouldn't learn anything."

"It's not your job to be my cooking instructor."

"It is if I ever expect you to prepare a meal for me."

Her hand stilled over the bowl. "I thought we'd settled that. There's not going to be anything personal between us."

"That would be the smart plan," he agreed, not entirely sure why he was so determined to pursue this. He was always, always smart. He skirted around mistakes at all costs, especially when they were staring him right in the face in a way that made them totally avoidable.

"It's the only plan," she insisted.

"Not really." He placed a hand over hers and guided it gently to the side of the bowl, then cracked the egg. It fell neatly into the bowl without so much as a sliver of shell. Melanie stared at it in obvious surprise.

"Now do that without my help," he instructed.

She broke another egg and then a third one, looking more incredulous each time she succeeded. "Well, I'll be darned." She gazed up at him. "Now what?"

"Now we add a little milk, a touch of vanilla, and whip it till it's frothy."

Clearly more confident, she reached for the milk and added a too-generous splash. She was a little too stingy with the vanilla, but he refrained from comment and handed her the whisk. She stared at it as if it were a foreign object. Richard bit back another smile. "You use it to whip the eggs."

"Why not a beater?"

"This is easier." He nudged her aside with his hip and took the whisk. "Like this."

She watched him closely, a little furrow of concentration knitting her brow. He couldn't help wondering if she was this intense about everything she did. Best not to go there.

"Now you do it," he said, handing the whisk back.

She tackled the task with more enthusiasm than finesse, but she got the job done with only a minimal amount of splashing. There was enough egg left in the bowl for at least a couple of pieces of French toast.

Hiding his amusement, Richard put some butter in a pan, then handed her the bread. "Dip it in the eggs till both sides are coated, then put it in the pan once the butter's melted. I'll get the syrup."

He turned away for no more than a few seconds, but that was long enough for her to manage to splatter her hand with the now-sizzling butter. He heard her curse and turned back to find her with tears in her eyes.

"Let me see," he commanded.

"It's nothing," she protested. "Just a little burn. I told you I'm hopeless in the kitchen."

"Not hopeless, just inexperienced. Sit down. I'll get some ointment for your hand."

"The French toast will be ruined," she argued.

"Then we'll make more." He took the pan off the burner, grabbed the first-aid kit, then pulled a chair up beside hers. "Let me see."

She held out her right hand, which already had a blister the size of a dime. He took her hand in his, trying not to notice how soft it was and how it seemed to fit so perfectly in his own. He put a little of the salve on the blister, but couldn't bring himself to release her hand. Instead, he waited until her head came up and her gaze met his.

"I'm sorry about last night," he apologized. "I never meant to make you uncomfortable. I don't even know why I said those things. I just wanted to push your buttons, I guess."

Temper immediately flashed in her eyes. "It was some kind of game? You didn't really want to sleep with me? I knew it. What kind of man are you?"

Uh-oh. That had definitely come out all wrong. "No," he said at once. "That's not it. Dammit, somehow whenever I'm with you, my words get all tangled up."

"I seem to have the same difficulty," she admitted with obvious reluctance.

He wanted to be sure she understood. "I do want you, but I also respect what you were saying about not getting involved with a client or even a prospective client. Besides, it's not as if we know each other well enough for me to haul you off to bed. That's not a step two people should take on impulse."

"No," she agreed softly.

He risked another look into her eyes. The temper had faded, replaced by heat of another kind entirely. She lifted her uninjured hand and touched his cheek.

"Impulses are a risky thing," she said.

"Melanie." His voice sounded choked.

"Yes, Richard."

"It's still a bad idea. You were right about that."

"I know," she said, but her hand continued to rest against his cheek.

"I still want to kiss you," he murmured honestly, aware that he was testing the waters, waiting for a response. When she didn't protest or back away, the last of his resolve vanished. "Ah, hell," he whispered, reaching for her.

She tasted of mint-flavored toothpaste and coffee. It wasn't a combination he would normally have found the slightest bit seductive, but right this second it struck him as heavenly. He wanted more.

Her lips were as soft and clever as he'd dreamed about during the long, lonely night. Her tongue was downright wicked.

But even as his senses whirled and his blood heated, his conscience wouldn't stay silent. A nagging voice kept asking him what the hell he thought he was doing. Seducing the sexiest woman to cross his path in months did not strike him as an adequate answer. It certainly wouldn't hold up to a grilling by his aunt, who was this woman's friend. Destiny might have a plan for the two of them, but he was relatively confident this wasn't it.

Eventually he let the voice in his head win, releasing Melanie reluctantly and sitting back on his chair, his hands clenched together as if he didn't quite trust them to do what his head told them to do.

"Sorry," he murmured.

"I kissed you back," she said honestly.

He grinned at her determined attempt to be fair. It was not an attitude he especially deserved, and they both knew it. "True enough," he said anyway, because he liked putting some heat into her eyes.

"You don't have to gloat," she grumbled.

He held up his hands. "Not gloating," he swore solemnly.

She regarded him with an intense, unsmiling expression. "Richard, just so you know, nothing's changed. I still won't sleep with you and I still want that contract.''

Richard didn't doubt either claim. He just wasn't sure he could live with them. Worse, he didn't know why the devil that was, which meant mistakes could start piling up before he figured it out if he didn't watch himself around her every single second. The trouble with that plan was that he much preferred simply watching her.

Chapter Four

Still feeling shaky from Richard's unexpected and thoroughly devastating kiss, Melanie retreated to the living room immediately after breakfast. She grabbed a legal pad and pen and settled in front of the warm fire, determined to get some work done for some of her more appreciative clients. She had plenty of challenges on her plate. She didn't need a stubborn man who wasn't interested in listening to her advice.

Despite her best efforts to concentrate, though, her mind wandered back to that kiss. No matter how hard she tried to steer her thoughts to something productive, she kept coming back to the way Richard's mouth had felt on hers, the way he'd managed to make her blood sing without half-trying. She found herself doodling little hearts like some schoolgirl with a crush. This was bad, really bad. Annoyed with herself, she impatiently flipped the page, cursing when it tore.

"Having trouble concentrating?"

She jumped at the sound of his voice, then scowled at the teasing note in it. "No."

He laughed. "I won't call you on that. However, since I can't seem to concentrate, either, I was going to suggest that we go for a walk and grab some lunch in town."

"We just had breakfast."

Richard gestured toward his watch. "Four hours ago," he noted. "You really have been drifting off, haven't you? What were you daydreaming about?" He gave her an amused, knowing look, then added, "Or were you fine-tuning your PR plan for me in case I decide to relent and let you present it?"

He reached for her legal pad with a motion so quick and sneaky, he managed to get it away from her. When he saw the hearts she'd drawn, he grinned.

Melanie wondered if it was possible to die of embarrassment. If so, now would be the perfect time for the floor of this place to open and swallow her up.

"Actually I was thinking about this really sexy television reporter I met last week," she lied boldly, thankful that she hadn't scribbled any initials on the page to give herself away and confirm the obvious conclusion he'd leaped to. That would have been totally humiliating. At least now he could only guess where her mind had been drifting. He couldn't prove a thing.

Richard took the bait, regarding her with curiosity. "Which reporter?"

"What difference does it make?"

"Just wondering about your taste in men," he claimed.

She didn't buy that for a second. Her taste in men was the last thing on his mind. He was just trying to trip her up. She named the most eligible bachelor on any of the news teams in town. He was an insipid bore, but maybe Richard wouldn't know that.

Unfortunately, he lifted a brow at her response. "Really? Everyone tells me he's pretty, but not too bright."

There was no mistaking the derisiveness in his voice. That "pretty" label sealed it.

Melanie refused to be daunted by his attitude. "Maybe I'm not interested in holding a conversation with him," she suggested.

Richard merely laughed. "You're going to have to do better than that, sweetheart. One rule of thumb when you're lying, you have to make it believable."

"I'm not surprised you know that," she muttered.

He ignored the gibe. "Come on, kiddo. On your feet. The exercise will clear your head, maybe get all those hot thoughts of your young stud muffin out of your brain."

Melanie sighed. He was right about one thing—she really did need a blast of cold air. Maybe then she'd stop making an idiot out of herself. It was not the best way to get Richard to take her work seriously.

Richard couldn't recall the last time he'd gone for a walk in the snow just for the sheer fun of it. Of course, in this case it was also a way to get out of the house and away from those wayward thoughts he was having about the impossible woman staying with him. The fact that she'd tried to sell him a bill of goods about that insipid reporter suggested she was aware that the temptation was getting too hot to handle, too.

Outside, though, the air was crisp and cold off the river. The sky, now that the storm had ended, was a brilliant blue. The sun made the drifts of white snow glisten as if the ground had been scattered with diamonds. He was glad he'd thought to put on his sunglasses. Of course, the almost childlike excitement shining in Melanie's eyes was just as blinding, and the glasses couldn't protect him from that.

When they'd left the house, she'd been totally guarded, most likely because of his teasing. Now all of that seemed to be forgotten. Every two feet, she paused to point out some Christmas-card-perfect scene.

"Look," she said in a hushed voice, grabbing his sleeve. "A cardinal."

Richard followed the direction of her gaze and found the cardinal, its red feathers a brilliant splash of color against the snow, a holly tree as its backdrop. Its less colorful mate was sitting on a tree branch, almost hidden by the dark green leaves and red berries. The birds were common, but Melanie made it seem as if this were something totally special and incredible. Her enthusiasm was contagious.

Melanie sighed. "I wish I had my camera."

"We can pick up one of that throwaway kind at the store," he suggested.

She looked at him as if he'd had a divine inspiration. "Now?" she asked with so much eagerness that he laughed.

"You are so easy to please," he teased. "A cheap camera and you're a pushover."

"I've decided to go with the flow today," she informed him.

Now there was a notion he could get behind. "Oh, really?"

She frowned at him in mock despair. "Not that flow," she scolded.

He shrugged. "Just a thought."

She gave him an odd look. "It's not as if you really want to seduce me," she said with surprising certainty. "So why do you say things like that?"

"What makes you think I don't want to seduce you?" In truth, the idea had been growing in appeal by leaps and bounds.

"You've admitted as much," she reminded him. "Not that I think you'd turn me down if I agreed to take you up on it, but you're really flirting to annoy me."

Richard wondered about that. He seemed to be taking the idea more and more seriously by the minute. Melanie wasn't his type, but there was something about her, something refreshingly honest and open and enthusiastic. He couldn't recall the last time he'd encountered that particular combination, much less been drawn to it. Maybe Destiny was right about that much, at least. Maybe he was ready for a change in his life, a spark of excitement and a few heady thrills. It would beat the mundane existence he'd been telling himself he was perfectly contented with.

He glanced at Melanie, noting the expectant look on her face as she awaited a reply to her challenge. "Maybe I am trying to annoy you," he agreed. "Then again, perhaps I'm just trying to prepare you for the moment when I make my first totally irresistible move."

She blinked at that, but then a smile broke across her face. "I don't think so," she said with complete confidence.

Vaguely disgruntled by her conviction, he asked, "Why not?"

"Because you don't play games. You take life far too seriously to be bothered with them."

His gaze narrowed. "Destiny's theory again?"

"No, my own personal observation," Melanie assured him. "I'm a good judge of people. That makes me an excellent public relations person, because I know how to make the public see what I see."

Richard was more curious than he'd expected to be about her perceptions. "What would you make them see about me? Not that I'm stuffy, I hope."

"No, I'd emphasize that you do take responsibility seriously, that you've worked hard at Carlton Industries and would work just as hard for your constituents. Those are good, solid recommendations for a candidate."

"I thought you didn't think I'd be a viable candidate because I hadn't walked in the shoes of those who've struggled," he reminded her.

She shrugged. "Maybe you convinced me otherwise."

"Or maybe you want this contract so badly, you're willing to say whatever it takes to get it," he said with an edge of cynicism.

She stopped in her tracks and scowled at him. "If you believe that, then you don't know me very well," she said, sounding genuinely miffed. "I don't work for anyone I don't believe in."

"You don't know me well enough to believe in me," he countered.

"Actually, I think I do. After your aunt suggested we meet, I did a lot of research before I agreed. I talked to people. I read everything in print. I wanted to be sure that Destiny wasn't being totally biased about your capabilities or your honesty and integrity. She wasn't. You're a good man, Richard. The consensus on that is unanimous." She gave him a considering look. "Whether you have what it takes to win an election is something else entirely."

Richard bristled at the suggestion that he wasn't up to the challenge of running for office or winning. "What is it you think I might be lacking?"

"An open mind," she said at once.

He started to argue, then saw exactly the trap she'd laid for him. "Because I made up my mind about hiring you before we'd even met," he guessed.

"That's one reason," she agreed. "And because now that we have met, you can't divorce my professional capabilities from the fact that I'm a woman who rattles you."

"You don't rattle me," he claimed, doubting whether he sounded the least bit convincing.

She regarded him with amusement. "There's the first real lie I've heard cross your lips."

"That you know of," he said, not denying that he'd lied in that instance. She did rattle him, no question about it. He'd just hoped to convince her otherwise. The woman saw too darn much. He didn't like it that she could get into his head. He prided himself on keeping most people off guard and at a distance. That kind of safety suited his comfort level.

"The first lie," she insisted.

Richard sighed. "Okay, say you're right about that.

Say I'm addicted to telling the truth *and* that you rattle me, so what?''

"Now we're getting somewhere," she said more cheerfully.

He stared at her in confusion. "Where?"

"You're very close to admitting that you've been mule-headed and stubborn and that you will read my business proposal when we get back to the cottage."

He regarded her incredulously. "You got that out of my admission?"

She grinned. "Brilliant, aren't I?"

He laughed despite himself. "Not necessarily brilliant, but sneaky. You're a lot like my aunt, in fact."

"I'll take that as a compliment."

He sighed. "To be honest, I'm not sure you should."

Melanie was feeling confident and in control when they sat down to lunch at a small café in the center of town. She was finally making progress. Maybe coming all the way down here hadn't been such a harebrained idea, after all. If she'd done this well before the man had even eaten, just think what she could accomplish once a crab-cake sandwich, some coleslaw and homemade apple cobbler with ice cream had improved his mood.

He gave her an odd look as she ordered the hearty lunch, then chuckled. "Trying to ply me with food, so I'll be in a more receptive frame of mind?"

"It did occur to me," she said. "Of course, you don't have to have what I'm having. And lunch is on me, by the way. I'm wooing a prospective client."

"I'm buying," he contradicted for the waitress's benefit. "As for the meal, I have to have what you're having if I expect to have the energy to keep up with you." He gave the amused waitress a conspiratorial wink. "Same thing for me, along with the strongest coffee you have."

The older woman grinned. "Honey, we don't serve it any other way."

"Too bad you're not running for office here," Melanie said when the woman had gone to place their order. "You'd have her vote locked up."

Richard sighed. "It's not supposed to be about charisma."

"It's not supposed to be, but it is, at least in part," she argued. "A dull man with a good message *can* get elected—it's just harder. You have both. Why not capitalize on it, instead of pretending that one thing doesn't matter?"

"In other words, I'm not going to get out of kissing babies and shaking hands," he said.

"Few politicians get elected without doing both," she said. "People want to see that the man they're electing is real, that he's human. They like to look him in the eye and gauge for themselves whether he's honest. They like to know that his handshake's firm."

Funny thing about that, Richard thought, falling silent. More than once he'd been accused of not being human—by competitors faced with his hard, cold stare during negotiations, by women who'd hoped for more from their relationship. He'd come to accept that there was something missing inside him, some connection he'd lost when his parents had died. Once, he'd despaired of ever getting that piece of himself back, but now, looking at Melanie, feeling her vitality and warmth touching him, he had a feeling he might be able to get it if only he reached out.

Then he immediately shook off the fanciful notion.

Melanie was here for one reason and one reason only, to strike a deal with him. Not to heal him. Like so many others, she simply wanted something from him. He didn't dare lose sight of that, despite the fact that he'd managed to veer her away from her mission on more than one occasion since her arrival.

Her fingers skimmed lightly across the back of his hand, startling him.

"Hey," she said softly, her expression puzzled, "where'd you go?"

"Back to reality," he said grimly.

Before she could ask the question that was so obviously on the tip of her tongue, their lunches came. Richard had never been so relieved by the sight of food in his life. He bit into his crab-cake sandwich with enthusiasm, but noted that it was some time before Melanie finally picked hers up, as if she couldn't quite get past his sudden shift of mood and all the questions it raised.

Once she'd tasted the crab-cake, though, her attention was totally focused on the sandwich. "Terrific crab, don't you think?"

He nodded. "Even out of season and frozen, it's delicious. Better than any I've had at some of the finest seafood places in Washington."

"Wonder what that spice is?" she mused, taking another taste. "It gives it a little kick."

"Given your avowed inability to cook, what difference does it make?"

"For something this good, I could learn," she insisted. "I'm not totally hopeless."

"Why bother, when you can just come here?"

"It's not like I get down this way all the time," she said. "In fact, I've never been to this part of Virginia before."

"Now that you know about the crab cakes, I'll bet you'll be back," he said. "Who knows, maybe I'll even invite you."

"I could probably starve before that happens," she said. "Maybe they'd ship them up to me. Even I could be trusted to cook them, if they're already prepared." Her expression turned wistful. "It would be so nice not to eat every meal out, at least if I want anything edible. Nuking a frozen dinner doesn't do it for me, except in an emergency."

Richard could relate to that. He ate far too many of his own meals at his desk or in restaurants, except on those occasions when Destiny commanded his presence at her table. She was an excellent cook, when she took the time to do it, and it had spoiled him for anything less than the best. The conversation around her table was also lively and challenging, even when it was a simple family meal with his two brothers. They didn't get together for those meals nearly often enough anymore. He needed to change that.

Funny how he recalled the laughter more than the actual food on the table. It had been good, but it was being with the three of them that he missed the most. He hadn't realized how lonely his life had become until just this moment. Not that he didn't see Destiny or talk to her almost daily and his brothers almost that often, but it wasn't the same as it had been when they'd all lived under one roof.

Sighing heavily, he gazed at Melanie. "Tell me about your family," he coaxed.

She stared at him as if he'd asked her to reveal her deepest secrets. "My family?"

"Yes. Big? Small? Where are they?"

"I have two older sisters, both married, both totally unambitious and disgustingly content with their husbands and kids. They still live in Ohio, within a few miles of our folks. They all pester me about my solitary lifestyle. They don't get it.''

''Were you close?''

She smiled. ''As close as three girls can be when they're fighting over the same dress to wear to a dance.''

''Do you envy them? What they have now?''

''At times,'' she admitted, her expression thoughtful. ''I love what I do and I am ambitious, but that doesn't mean I don't wish I had someone to share it with.''

Her thoughts so closely mirrored what Richard had been thinking only moments before, it made him sigh again. ''I know what you mean,'' he admitted with rare candor.

Melanie regarded him with surprise. ''You do?''

''Sure. What's the thrill of conquering the world, if there's no one to tell, no one who'll get excited about it?''

''Exactly,'' she said at once. ''It doesn't mean we're dissatisfied with what we have or that we're ungrateful, just that we recognize that there can be more. That's a good thing, don't you think?''

''Self-awareness is always good, or so they say.''

''So, if you know there's something lacking in your life, why haven't you married any of those women with whom you've been involved?'' she asked.

Richard shuddered. ''Because I couldn't imagine bringing a single one of them into a place like this for a crab cake and homemade apple cobbler.''

Melanie's expression softened. ''Really?''

''Yes,'' he said. ''But don't let it go to your head.''

''Of course not,'' she said at once.

"And it doesn't mean I'll think about hiring you," he added for good measure.

"I know that," she agreed, but she looked a little smug.

"It just means that you remind me a lot of Destiny," he explained, trying to sort through his feelings even as he attempted to explain them to her. "You're outspoken and unpredictable and..." He faltered.

"Open to new ideas?" she suggested.

Richard laughed. "Don't push it."

"But people who are open to new ideas aren't—"

"Stuffy," he supplied before she could say it. "I know. I get it."

She studied him intently. "Do you really?"

"Yes," he assured her.

"Then maybe we should go back to the cottage," she suggested.

"So I can read your proposal?"

"That, too, but I was also thinking of getting totally wild and letting you kiss me again."

Richard stared at her, bemused by the outrageous suggestion. "Why would you do that?"

"Because I have an open mind."

"Which means seduction could be back on the table?" he asked, wanting to be sure he got it exactly right before he made a damn fool out of himself. He hadn't wanted a woman as badly as he wanted Melanie Hart in so long, he wasn't sure he could trust his own instincts.

"You never know," she said with a shrug.

"I think you need to be clearer than that," he said, as he tossed a handful of bills on the table to pay for lunch, then grabbed his coat.

"What fun is life, if everything has to be spelled out ahead of time?"

He frowned at her. "It may be more fun, but my way averts disaster."

She accepted his help with her coat, then faced him, her expression totally serious. "Okay, then, here it is. Not that I'm crazy about it, but right now, this minute, I want you to kiss me again. I am still opposed to anything more happening between us, because it could get messy, especially if I wind up working for you."

"I see," he said.

"However," she added, then grinned, "I might be open to persuasion."

His pulse kicked up at the tiny opening.

"Maybe not today," she added pointedly. "Maybe not tomorrow. But the future could hold all sorts of surprises."

Despite the fact that she'd pretty much told him he was going to go to bed frustrated tonight and possibly for many nights to come, Richard couldn't seem to help whistling as they walked outside into the cold air.

Melanie frowned at him. "You seem awfully chipper for a man who's just been told he's not going to have sex."

He laughed. "Is that what you said?"

"I certainly thought it was."

"Not what I heard," he said. "I heard that there would be no sex *tonight,* but that tomorrow—as a very famous fictional Southern belle once said—most definitely is another day." He took her hand and kissed it. "I'm a very patient man. Was that in that research of yours?"

She regarded him with a vaguely shaken expression. "I thought I was very thorough, but I must have missed that."

"Keep it in mind. It could be important," he told her, then scooped up some snow and pelted her with it. Best to cool them both down for the moment, he thought.

Eyes wide, she stared at him in shock for fully a minute before her eyes filled with that fire he'd come to crave.

"You are so dead," she said, bending down to make a soft snowball of her own.

"I doubt that," Richard said, not even bothering to run.

"You don't think I'll throw this at you?"

"Oh, I think you'll throw it," he said, then grinned. "I just think you'll miss."

Even as he started moving, she hauled off and managed to hit him lightly on one cheek.

"Bad move, darlin'," he said, coming back for her, even as she frantically scooped up more and more snow and threw it with dead-on accuracy. He had her off her feet and on her backside in a deep drift of snow before she realized what he intended.

Sputtering with indignation, she stared up at him and then started laughing. Only when he was laughing right along with her did she snag his ankle, give him a jerk and land him on his butt right beside her.

Richard didn't waste time protesting her sneakiness. The snow was cold as the dickens. Only one way he could think of to counteract that. He rolled over and caught her, then captured her mouth under his. He'd hoped for a little heat, but he got a full-fledged blaze. Apparently she didn't hold a grudge.

Of course, if she also stuck to her resolve about keeping sex out of the equation, at least for tonight, it was going to be a very long time till morning.

Chapter Five

Okay, maybe it was freezing cold out, but that was no reason for her to be playing with fire, Melanie thought, as she gazed into Richard's turbulent eyes. They were filled with the kind of stormy emotions she hadn't expected at all, not from a man reputed to have no heart.

She'd been counting on that reputation for being distant when she'd agreed to see him the very first time. She'd known from looking at his pictures that he'd appeal to her physically. She'd known from listening to Destiny that his tragic early years would pluck at her heartstrings. But she was not normally drawn to arrogance or to men who were emotionally shut down. She'd figured those two traits would keep her safe.

After their first meeting, when those traits had been evident in spades, she'd been comforted. Now this…

Forget his heart, she commanded. Where was her head? Had her brain cells frozen on the walk back to the cottage? Is that why she'd been tossing out taunting comments about kisses and sex and then rolling around in the snow with Richard? Those were definitely not in her business plan.

Before she made a mistake they would both regret, she leaped up and brushed herself off, then faced him as if nothing the least bit provocative had been going on, not in the restaurant, not now. "You surprise me," she said lightly. "I would never have imagined you loosening up enough to play around in the snow like some kid."

He rose, looking too blasted dignified, his expression completely sober. "Yes, well, I imagine despite all that research of yours, I still have a few surprises left."

Melanie sighed at the return of his straitlaced demeanor. She was beginning to think it was nothing more than self-protective armor, and that made her weak-kneed all over again. "Richard, I'm sorry, but what just went on here?"

He shrugged. "I suppose, for a couple of minutes, both of us lost track of why we're together."

"In other words, we were behaving like a male and female who are attracted to each other, rather than prospective business associates," she said. "I'm sorry."

"Not your fault. I'm the one who's sorry for crossing a line."

"But I invited you to cross it."

He scowled at her. "Quit being so damned reasonable," he muttered. "There's no way this weekend could have anything other than a bad ending."

Melanie felt worse than ever. For a few minutes Richard had forgotten himself, pushed aside his responsibilities and found his long-lost inner child. He'd revealed his human side. Then she'd gone and ruined that by getting too uptight and serious. Of course, if she apologized one more time, he was liable to blow sky-high. He seemed to be operating on a very short fuse. It would have been a good time to get out of town, but unfortunately the local roads had yet to be cleared.

She held out her hand, determined to get them back on a safer footing. "Truce?"

He gave her a mocking look. "I hadn't realized we were at war."

"But we're heading in that direction," she said. "And it *is* my fault. I sent out all sorts of mixed messages."

He gazed into her eyes, his expression forbidding. "Maybe it would be smarter to stay at odds," he suggested. "We don't seem to be able to handle anything else without getting offtrack."

It was true, though Melanie couldn't imagine why that was. Forget all the issues about working with him, he was far too intense—okay, far too stuffy—to be attractive to her, beyond his obvious physical appeal. And yet he *was* attractive, no question about that. Otherwise she wouldn't have come so darn close to throwing herself at him without one second's consideration of her deeply held principles about mixing business and pleasure.

She imagined that he found the whole attraction thing to be just as confusing. She was nothing at all like the rich, sophisticated, edgy women with whom he was normally seen around town. She'd seen him in black tie often enough on the society pages to recognize the glamorous type of woman he preferred.

Given that, there was only one thing to do. If they both accepted the notion of anything personal between them being insane, then perhaps the next few hours wouldn't be too awful. In fact, perhaps by morning they'd be able to laugh about everything, shake hands and say goodbye with no lingering regrets. She'd write off any chance of landing this PR consulting contract and cut her losses. Anything else would be complete lunacy.

Even as she was coming to that conclusion, Richard reached into his jacket and pulled out a key. "Why don't you go on back to the house?" he suggested, offering it to her.

"Where are you going?" she asked as she accepted the key and tucked it into her own jacket pocket.

"For a walk," he said. "I'll pick up one of those cameras for you."

Melanie opened her mouth to offer to come with him, but he'd already turned on his heel and taken off. Clearly he was eager to escape her company. This was what she'd wanted not five seconds ago, but now she was having second thoughts.

She heaved a sigh as she watched him go, shoulders hunched against the wind that had kicked up off the river. He looked so alone. How was it possible that a man as rich, brilliant and sexy as Richard Carlton could be so completely alone?

She had answers to all sorts of questions about him stored away in her research files, but not to that one. Naturally that meant it was the one she found most intriguing, the one that opened a tiny little place in her heart to him.

And that, she concluded with complete candor, was the one that could prove to be her undoing.

Richard knew it was ridiculous to feel cranky and completely out of sorts because a woman had changed her mind—and the rules—on him. It happened all the time, and he'd never given two figs about it before. Women were unpredictable creatures, that was all. It wasn't personal. He'd watched Destiny dispatch so many perfectly respectable suitors over the years, he'd come to accept the behavior as normal.

But he'd taken Melanie's sudden change of heart damn personally, which meant that on some totally unexpected level she'd gotten to him. How the devil had that happened?

He wrestled with that unanswerable question all the way to the fast-mart, where he picked up a disposable camera, then had a sudden inspiration to buy a just-released video and some popcorn for that evening. If they were going to be stuck here together for another night, entertainment that didn't require conversation seemed like a fine idea.

As he trudged back toward the cottage through the deep snow, he tried to recapture some of his earlier delight in the quiet, snow-shrouded landscape, but it wouldn't come. Without Melanie, it was a bit as if that cardinal had flown away, taking all of the color with it.

He groaned at the thought. He did not want Melanie Hart adding color to his life. He didn't want to start waxing poetic about her influence on him or his surroundings. He wanted to go back to that serene time earlier in the week before he'd ever met the annoying woman. Then the prospect of several uninterrupted hours in front of his computer or with his mountain of paperwork would have been the bright spot on his weekend agenda.

Unfortunately, recapturing that serenity was all but impossible when Melanie was going to be underfoot the second he crossed the threshold at the cottage. And she would be underfoot. She seemed to be the kind who liked to talk things out, make perfect sense of them, instead of accepting that they'd nearly made a dreadful mistake and moving on. He'd seen that let's-talk-about-this look in her eyes right before he'd turned on his heel and left her a few blocks from the cottage. He hoped to hell she was over it by now.

He was half-frozen by the time he reached the cottage. He was grateful for the blazing fire she'd started, but as he waited for Melanie to appear, to start pestering him with comments or analysis or, God forbid, yet another apology, he grew increasingly perplexed by her absence. Had she taken off, even though the local roads were still all but impassable? Come to think of it, had he paid any attention to whether her car was still in the driveway? He couldn't remember noticing.

Panicked that she might have done something so completely impulsive and dangerous because of him, he bounded upstairs and very nearly broke down the guest-room door with his pounding. He heard her sleepily mumbled "What?" just as he threw open the door.

Undisguised relief flooded through him at the sight of her in the bed, the comforter pulled up to her chin, her hair rumpled, her eyes dazed.

"Is something wrong?" she asked in that same husky, half-asleep tone.

The comforter drooped, revealing one bare shoulder and a tantalizing hint of breast. Heart pounding, Richard began backing away. "No, really. Sorry."

"Richard?"

Even half-asleep, she was constitutionally incapable of letting anything go, he concluded grimly. He was going to have to explain himself, or at least come up with something plausible that wouldn't give away how frantic he'd been when he'd imagined her risking her neck on the icy roads.

"Um, the front door was open," he said, improvising quickly. "I thought someone might have broken in. I just wanted to be sure you were okay."

Her gaze narrowed. "The front door was open?"

"Just a crack," he said, guessing that she was about to worry that piece of information to death.

"But I closed it. I know I did. I didn't lock it, because I wasn't sure if you had another key with you and I wasn't sure if I'd hear you if I fell asleep and you knocked, but I'm sure it was securely shut."

"No big deal," he said. "As long as you're okay. Go back to sleep. Sorry I disturbed you."

She smiled and stretched, allowing another tiny slip of the comforter. She seemed to be oblivious to the sexy picture she presented.

"I'm awake now. I might as well get up."

Because she seemed about to do exactly that without regard for her lack of attire—or what his vivid imagination believed to be her lack of attire—Richard bolted. He wasn't sure his heart could take the image of a totally unclad Melanie being burned in his mind forever.

He was downstairs, in the kitchen, making another pot of very strong coffee, when she finally appeared, her face scrubbed clean, her hair tidied. He'd liked it better all tousled, but it was evident she was trying to reclaim her professional—totally untouchable—decorum. He could have told her that not even the most modest power suit of all time could accomplish that. She was an innately sexy woman, the kind who conjured up forbidden images, at least for him.

"Coffee?" he offered.

"No, thanks. Too much caffeine and I'll never sleep tonight."

Richard was pretty sure he wasn't going to sleep anyway, so a little caffeine wasn't going to matter. "I bought a video for us to watch later," he said, gesturing to the table.

She picked it up, studied it, then grinned. "You bought a romantic comedy?"

"I heard it was good," he muttered defensively. "I thought all women liked that kind of sappy stuff."

"We do. I'm just surprised you took my feelings into account."

"My aunt raised me to be a thoughtful host."

"Even when you're an unwilling one?" she asked skeptically.

"Even then," he insisted. "Maybe it's most important of all then. And Destiny obviously knew that I'd mastered that lesson when she sent you charging down here. Otherwise, she wouldn't have risked it."

Melanie met his gaze and opened her mouth. Richard cut her off. "I don't want to hear another apology. We both know you're here because of my aunt. If anyone's to blame for the awkwardness of the situation, it's Destiny."

"She was just trying to help both of us out," Melanie replied. "You can hardly blame her for caring about you and for trying to do me a favor."

"Yes, I can," he said grimly. "When it takes the form of meddling, I most certainly can. If this was only about that contract, she'd have planted you in my office on Monday morning, not in this cottage on a Friday night, armed with my favorite wine and food."

Melanie grimaced. "Maybe we shouldn't go there. We don't seem to see eye-to-eye on your aunt's motivation. In fact, maybe I should go in the living room and sit in front of the fire and get some work done, and you can stay in here and do the same."

Richard bit back a grin. "Retreating to neutral corners, as it were."

"Exactly."

"Maybe that's not such a bad idea," he said as he gazed directly into her eyes. He thought he detected a faint hint of longing there. Best not to give himself the chance to discover if he was right.

She stood there, looking undecided, then finally sighed. "See you later, then."

"Yeah, see you later." When she was almost out of sight, he called after her. "Melanie?"

She hesitated but didn't turn back to face him. "Yes?"

"Anything in particular you'd like for dinner?"

She turned then, her expression perplexed. "There are choices?"

"Sure. Why would you think otherwise?"

"Destiny made it seem as if…"

"As if I would be starving if you didn't show up down here," Richard guessed. He grinned. "Told you what she was up to."

Melanie nodded. "Damn but she's good," she said, sounding more admiring than annoyed.

"It's something we should both keep in mind, don't you think?" he responded.

"Oh, yes," she said, squaring her shoulders. "I will definitely keep that in mind. As for dinner, surprise me."

As if I could, Richard thought, but he nodded. Maybe when it came to dinner, he could come up with something totally unexpected. Lord knew, though, that the woman seemed able to read his mind when it came to anything else.

Melanie grabbed her cell phone and marched outside, oblivious to the cold. She punched in Destiny Carlton's number, then waited for a connection. When it came, the signal was faint, but she could hear Destiny's cheerful voice.

"You are one very sneaky woman," Melanie accused, though without too much rancor.

"Melanie, darling. How are you? Are you stranded down there with Richard?" There was an unmistakably optimistic note in her voice.

"I'm sure you knew I would be," Melanie grumbled.

"Not knew, *hoped,*" Destiny corrected. "Is it going well? Has he agreed to hire you yet?"

"No."

"Oh," Destiny said, clearly disappointed. "Maybe I should have a talk with him. Where is he?"

"In the kitchen working, and I am not letting you talk to him," Melanie said. "I think you've done quite enough meddling for one weekend."

"Has something gone wrong?" Destiny asked worriedly. "You two haven't had words, have you?"

"Not the way you mean. What we *have* done is compare notes. Now I'm even more suspicious of your motives than I was the other day. In fact, I'm convinced that your intentions were not entirely aboveboard and honorable."

"That's a fine thing to say when I've only been trying to help you out," Destiny said with indignation.

"Nice try," Melanie retorted, not buying the huffy act for an instant. "And I'm sure that getting me this contract is at least a small part of what you're after, but you want more out of this weekend, don't you?"

"I have no idea what you're suggesting," the older woman claimed blithely. "Whoops, there's my other line. I'm expecting an important call from Richard's brother Mack. Have a lovely time down there, darling, and give Richard a kiss for me. Don't you two dare leave until the roads are cleared. I don't want to be worried sick that you're skidding into a snowdrift."

She was gone before Melanie could respond. Give the man a kiss for her, Melanie thought irritably. Right. That was exactly what Destiny was after, and the more kissing the better. She punched in Destiny's number again, but this time the connection wouldn't go through at all. Melanie sighed, jammed the cell phone back in her pocket and went inside.

Richard walked into the living room just then and regarded her quizzically. "What on earth were you doing outside without a coat?"

"Calling your aunt."

His lips twitched. "And?"

"She denies that this was a setup for anything other than getting a business deal worked out."

"What did you expect, that she'd admit to it?"

"Yes, I expected her to be honest."

"I'm sure she was. In fact, I imagine if you went over every word that came out of her mouth, you wouldn't find a single thing that wasn't accurate and truthful."

Melanie considered the conversation she'd just had with the maddening woman and concluded Richard was right. Destiny had skirted carefully around any outright lies, while admitting nothing. "She should be the one going into politics," she muttered.

"Heaven help us if she chose to," Richard said. "She doesn't suffer fools gladly, and the political arena is crawling with idiots. Destiny's completely nonpartisan when it comes to calling it as she sees it. After a few weeks, no political party would have her."

"Just think how refreshing it would be to listen to her, though," Melanie speculated.

"Refreshing is not the word I would have chosen," Richard replied. "But, then, I've been listening to her most of my life and have seen what she's like once she gets a bee in her bonnet. She's relentless."

"And you think that's what we are, a bee in her bonnet?"

"I'd stake my life on it."

"Well, too bad," Melanie said forcefully. "She's just going to have to lose this one. You and I have agreed on that."

She looked up to find Richard staring at her, that disconcerting heat once again blazing in his eyes.

"Have we really?" he asked softly.

Her pulse leaped. "Yes, of course, we have," she said, trying hard to sound irrefutably emphatic.

"Then Destiny will just have to accept it," he said, with what sounded like a vague note of regret in his voice.

Melanie swallowed hard, trying not to choke on her own regrets. "Suddenly I'm starving," she said. "Must be all that fresh air and exercise."

Richard finally tore his gaze away. "I'll start dinner then. Would you like a glass of wine? There's another bottle of cabernet."

"Sure," she said eagerly. One glass would calm her nerves. And one was her limit. Two would weaken her resolve, and it was already nearly in tatters.

She followed Richard into the kitchen. "Do you think we'll be able to get away from here in the morning?"

"The main roads will definitely be clear, and I imagine even that insubstantial little car of yours will be able to get out to the highway."

He sounded almost as eager to put an end to this weekend as she was. If he mattered to her in a personal way, his words would have hurt her feelings. As it was, there was just a tiny little nip to her ego. Or so she told herself.

"Stay here while I cook," he suggested, his fingers lingering against hers as he handed her the glass of wine.

"Not a good idea," she said.

"Why?"

"You know the answer to that. We seem to lose our heads when we're in the same room for too long."

"And that's such a bad thing?"

"Richard!"

He shrugged. "I just thought it would be nice to have some company." He grinned. "I'll give you a knife, and you can cut the vegetables. If I get out of line, you can defend yourself."

Melanie laughed, despite all the warning bells going off in her head. She pulled out a chair and sat down at the kitchen table, taking a long swallow of wine. Then she met his gaze.

He looked surprisingly relieved.

"Thank you," he said.

"Whatever," she replied, then grinned. "But I want a very big knife."

"Now there's a sentence guaranteed to strike terror in a man's heart," he said, laughing even as he handed her a deadly looking butcher knife, then added a more suitable paring knife for the vegetables.

They managed to get through the dinner preparations without bloodshed and without a single sly innuendo or seductive comment. Part of Melanie was relieved by that. Another part of her felt as if she'd lost something important.

It was because of that part that she set her glass aside at the end of the meal and stood up. "I'll say good-night now," she told him.

"You don't want to see the movie?"

"I've seen it," she fibbed, because she couldn't risk letting her defenses down for one more second.

"Why didn't you say something earlier? I could have gone out and gotten another movie."

"Maybe you should watch this one," she told him. "The hero winds up with the girl."

She felt his gaze on her as she left the room and

DEEP'S MARKET
45 North St
Danbury, CT 06810
The road to a friend's house is
never long. #Spanish Proverb

Lane: 6 Trx: 645129 02/02/04 12:32
Checker 17

AMBASSADOR GIFT BAG   3.49 T
CHERRY PIE   2.99 F
HALLMARK PINK TISSUE   1.75 T
CELESTIAL DECAF MANDAR   2.59 F
GFIC SF/FAT FREE FR. V   3.99 F
G-FOODS CHAI LATTE TEA   3.99 F
FLORIST   4.99 T

          Sales Total: $23.83
CT 6% Sales Tax $0.62

          Total Due: $24.45

Cash $24.45

    Cash Change Due: $0.00
    From Our Family To Yours....
THANK YOU FOR SHOPPING WITH US !

knew he had gotten the message that he needed a few pointers if *he* was ever going to do the same. She wasn't sure why it seemed to matter so much to her that he understand that, but it was. And that was more troubling than anything else that had gone on all weekend long.

Chapter Six

Richard had stayed up till midnight watching the romantic comedy he'd bought. He'd heard the unspoken message in Melanie's parting shot the night before. The suggestion that he had no idea what women wanted, that he couldn't keep one, had rankled.

If he wanted a woman in his life, he'd have one. He'd achieved every other goal he'd set for himself. He didn't doubt for a second that he could have a wife if he wanted one. He'd simply chosen to remain single. Period.

He'd been tempted to follow Melanie upstairs and tell her that, but had managed to stop himself from making that mistake. A discussion with Melanie—in her bedroom no less—could not lead to anything but trouble.

Still, he had watched the movie. He hadn't much enjoyed watching the hero twist himself inside out trying to figure out how to win the heroine's heart. If that was what Melanie—or any other woman— wanted from a man, she was fresh out of luck with him.

After watching the end of the video, he'd gone to bed in a foul mood. And he was still feeling cranky and out of sorts when Melanie breezed downstairs in the morning looking fresh as a daisy. Obviously she hadn't lain awake all night grappling with any aspect of their relationship. Or, more precisely, their nonre- lationship.

"You look chipper," he said in a way that even he could hear made "chipper" into a less-than-positive thing.

"Feeling great," she concurred, ignoring his testy tone. "Is that bacon I smell?"

"Yes, and I have batter for waffles, if you want one," he offered.

"Heaven," she said as she poured herself a cup of coffee. "Did you sleep well?"

"Like a baby," he lied.

She gave him a doubtful look but didn't question his claim. "I noticed that the road in front of the house has been plowed. I'm sure you'll be relieved to have me out from underfoot and have this place back to yourself," she said. "I'll take off as soon as I've had something to eat."

Instead of cheering him up, her announcement made him want to dawdle. Because that was so com- pletely ridiculous, he immediately poured batter onto the steaming waffle iron and snapped the lid closed. He took the plateful of bacon he'd microwaved earlier out of the oven where he'd been keeping it warm, then slammed it down on the table with more force than necessary. Melanie gave him another questioning look but remained silent.

"Juice?" he asked. "There's orange." He peered into the refrigerator as if there were some uncertainty, then added, "And cranberry."

"Orange juice would be good," she said, watching him closely. Apparently she could no longer contain her curiosity, because she added with concern, "Richard, are you upset about something?"

"Absolutely not," he said sharply, in a tone guaranteed to contradict his words.

Melanie retreated into wounded silence, which was what he'd been hoping for—wasn't it? Instead, he felt like he'd kicked a friendly puppy.

"Sorry," he muttered. "Obviously I got out of bed on the wrong side this morning."

She shrugged. "Just proves you're human."

"Stop that! Stop letting me off the hook," he snapped, annoyed with her, with himself, with the universe.

She stared at him. "Okay, what's really going on here? Have I missed something? Did you want me to take off right away? Have I tested your patience long enough?"

Richard sighed. "No. It's not you. It's me. To be honest, I don't know what I want. Blame my lousy mood on stress, not enough sleep, whatever."

"You said you slept like a baby."

Naturally she'd been paying close attention to his stupid lie and just had to call him on it. He should have expected that. Frowning, he admitted, "I lied."

"Why?"

"Because you came in here all cheerful and bright eyed and I didn't want you to think I'd lost even a second's sleep last night." He kept his gaze firmly fixed on the waffle iron when he made the admission.

"Are we having some sort of competition?" she asked, sounding genuinely perplexed.

"My entire life has been about competition," he muttered, as he snagged the golden waffle, put it on a plate and placed it in front of her.

"With whom? Your brothers?"

He shook his head. "With myself. I set goals, mostly based on my father's expectations, then I battle with myself to attain them." He gave her a wry look. "So far I'm right on track."

"But are you happy?" she asked quietly.

"Of course," he said quickly, possibly too quickly.

Melanie kept her steady gaze on him and waited.

"Mostly," he amended finally. He'd been completely happy until he'd watched that ridiculous movie and started questioning the lack of a woman in his life.

"What do you win in these competitions of yours?"

"Respect," he said immediately.

"You mean self-respect."

Richard shook his head. "No, just respect."

She regarded him quizzically. "Your father's?" she asked, her voice incredulous. "Is that it, Richard? Are you still trying to earn your father's respect?"

As she said it, he heard how ridiculous that sounded. His father had been dead for twenty years. "That would be impossible," he said, shaken by the sudden awareness of what he'd been doing for far too long. He'd been living his life to please a man who could no longer be satisfied—or dissatisfied—with his accomplishments. And overnight he'd been examining his entire life based on a movie premise…and on one offhand comment from a woman who barely knew him.

"Yes," Melanie told him. "It would be. Self-respect is far more important, don't you think?"

This was more self-analysis than Richard could cope with on an empty stomach. "Enough of this," he said brusquely. "How's your waffle?"

Her gaze held his, challenged him, but then she finally let it drop to the forkful of waffle she was holding. "Perfect," she said. "You could always open a restaurant, if you get tired of running a multinational conglomerate."

"We have restaurants," he noted as he sat down with his own plate and poured maple syrup over the waffle.

She chuckled. "I doubt you've seen the inside of the kitchen in any of them."

Richard shrugged. "They have fine chefs and great managers. They don't need me in there. All I care about is the bottom line of that division."

"Adding up all those numbers is what gives you pleasure?" she prodded.

"Of course. It's what I do best. Numbers are logical."

"And that's important to you, isn't it? You need everything in your life to be logical."

He frowned at her. "You say that as if it's a crime."

"Not a crime," she said lightly. "Just not much fun."

How many times had he listened to exactly the same lecture from Destiny? It hadn't bothered him half as much when his aunt had tried to get through to him. "I have fun," he insisted.

"When?"

"All the time."

"Are you talking about all those charity balls you attend?"

He nodded. "Sure."

"Then why do you always look so miserable in the pictures they take for the papers?"

"Miserable?" he repeated, astonished. "I'm always smiling."

Melanie shook her head. "Not with your eyes," she told him. "That's where the truth is, you know, in the eyes."

Richard's gaze automatically sought out her eyes and saw compassion and warmth and even a hint of yearning. She was right. The truth was in the eyes. He wondered if she had any idea what message was shining in hers.

All he knew for certain was that the message scared him to death, because it so closely mirrored what he was trying so damn hard to hide.

"How did your weekend go?" Destiny inquired innocently on Monday morning when she put in one of her rare appearances in Richard's office.

He'd been expecting her today, though. He was ready for her, or at least he thought he was. "The house is still standing, if that's what you're asking. I came away without any broken bones."

"And Melanie?"

"I didn't strangle her." He gave his aunt a hard look. "What are you up to, Destiny? I know what you told Melanie, but I'm not buying the innocent act. I want the truth.''

"I'm trying to find you a good marketing person,'' his aunt claimed. "Did you even look at her proposal?''

He had. He'd studied it in the wee hours of Sunday morning when he'd been unable to sleep for thinking about the movie…and about Melanie's presence in the guest room. She was an annoying little chatterbox, but she'd been growing on him. The entire weekend he'd been able to think of only one way to shut her up. Since she'd ruled that out, she'd wisely scampered off to bed alone and he'd stayed up nursing the last of the wine while he watched that ridiculous comedy with its feel-good happy ending. When was real life ever like that?

Suddenly aware that Destiny was regarding him with an amused expression, he tried to focus on their conversation. "She has some interesting ideas,'' he conceded.

"Then hire her.''

"She's ditzy,'' he said, falling back on his original impression because recent impressions were far too complicated. "She'd drive me crazy in a week. Maybe less.'' He knew that for a fact, because she'd driven him crazy in just two days. She'd upended his need for logic and made him crave all sorts of things he'd never expected to need. She'd tapped into emotions he'd spent a lifetime avoiding.

"What's wrong with that?'' Destiny asked, her eyes filled with knowing laughter.

Richard cringed. It was almost as if Destiny had been an eyewitness to the way Melanie had rattled him and thoroughly approved of it. Maybe she was merely psychic. Whatever, if she got it into her head that her scheme was working, she'd never let up.

Before he could list all the things wrong with any kind of relationship with Melanie—business or otherwise—she said, "You need someone around to drive you crazy. Everyone else in your life bows to your every whim."

"You don't," he pointed out.

"Yes, but I'm your aunt. I might get on your nerves, but you cut me a lot of slack."

"I'll cut you a lot less now that you've sent Melanie into my life," he vowed.

She laughed, clearly unintimidated. "If you don't hire her, you'll regret it."

In Richard's opinion, if he didn't sleep with her, he'd regret that more, but he wasn't about to share that insight with his aunt. Especially since it was probably exactly what she'd had in mind in the first place when she arranged all of this.

He really needed to get on the phone with Mack and Ben and warn his brothers that their aunt was dedicating herself to playing matchmaker these days. If she tired of her lack of success with him, they were definitely next in line. He owed them the heads-up. Then, again, it might be more fun to let her take them by surprise, the way she'd sneaked up on him.

"Why don't you meddle in Mack's life?" he suggested hopefully. "Or Ben's?"

Destiny's eyes sparkled with merriment. "What makes you think I haven't?" she inquired blithely, then turned and sailed out of his office, leaving him speechless and not one bit closer to being off the hook.

* * *

Melanie stared glumly at the Carlton Industries folder on her desk. It had been such a wonderful opportunity for her, but the odds of Richard ever changing his mind and hiring her were so astronomical, she might as well run the folder through the shredder.

She was genuinely considering doing just that when Becky came in with two cups of latte and cranberry scones from the café down the street. She held them just out of Melanie's reach.

"If I give you these, will you tell me everything that went on between you and Richard Carlton this weekend?" she asked.

"No," Melanie said, snatching the coffee out of her friend's hand. She could live without the scone if she had to. Caffeine was another story.

"Testy, aren't you? It must not have gone very well."

"That depends on your definition of success," Melanie replied, taking her first sip of the heavenly latte. "He didn't toss me out in the snow."

"Interesting," Becky said with a thoughtful expression. "Then you were stranded there all weekend?"

"Yes."

"And with all that time on your hands, you couldn't convince him to hire you?"

"I never even convinced him to read the proposal," she admitted grimly. "I was just about to shred my copy and write the whole thing off as a loss."

Becky stared at her in shock. "What kind of defeatist attitude is that? You never give up."

"I do when the odds of winning are impossible."

Becky's gaze narrowed. "Did he seduce you?"

Melanie scowled at her. "No."

"Did he at least try?"

Melanie thought back over the weekend and the dance they'd played. Richard had tossed out a proposition, she'd dodged it, he'd parried, then she'd taken a turn muddying the waters. "It was a bit confusing," she said finally.

"Then he did try," Becky concluded. "And you what?"

"I said no, of course."

"And then?"

"What makes you think that wasn't the end of it?"

Becky gave her a knowing look. "It was a long weekend."

"Okay, then I threw myself at him."

"Interesting."

"No, stupid. I corrected the mistake almost immediately."

"Almost?"

"Soon enough," Melanie said. "I didn't sleep with him. In fact, I only kissed him once. No big deal."

"Oh, right. The sexiest, richest man in all of Alexandria, maybe in the entire Washington metropolitan region, kisses you, and it's no big deal."

Melanie sighed. "Okay, the kiss *was* a big deal, but that's as far as it went and it won't be happening again. He couldn't get me out of there fast enough yesterday morning."

"Probably because he was tempted," Becky concluded. "Men do that, you know. They act all weird and crazy when they're losing control."

Melanie heard something in Becky's voice, a faint catch, that hinted she was no longer talking about the weekend Melanie had just shared with a prospective client. "Something happen with you and Jason?" Jason was the love of Becky's life, or so she'd persuaded herself. He was the fourth one this year, but even Melanie was almost convinced he was a keeper.

Becky's eyes immediately clouded up. "We broke up. More precisely, he broke up with me."

That was new. Usually Becky was the one running for cover. Melanie tried to muster the appropriate amount of sympathy, which was getting harder and harder to do. It was somewhat easier with Jason, because she'd genuinely liked him. She'd even thought Becky had gotten it right for once. "Oh, sweetie, I'm so sorry. I know you thought he was the one."

"He is the one," Becky said fiercely. "He's just being stubborn and scared and stupid."

"It's really hard to argue with stubborn, scared and stupid," Melanie pointed out. "You should know. You've done it often enough yourself."

"But if it's what you want, you have to fight for it, right?"

"I suppose."

Becky gave her a challenging look. "Okay, then. I will if you will."

"Meaning?" Melanie asked cautiously.

"I'll keep fighting for what I have—what I want— with Jason, if you'll keep fighting for Richard."

"This isn't about Richard and me. What's going on with us isn't personal," Melanie replied irritably. "It's about the Carlton Industries contract."

Becky gave her a sympathetic look. "Oh, sweetie, it might have started that way, but it's taken on a whole new twist. I can see it in your eyes, hear it in your voice. The sooner you wake up and accept that, the better off you'll be."

"It's about the contract," Melanie insisted stubbornly.

"Fine. Whatever gets you to pick up the phone and call the man," Becky said.

"I will not call him. The ball's in his court."

"Not if you packed up all the balls and brought them with you when you left his house," Becky said, then sighed heavily. "Okay, never mind. I recognize that tone. I'll stop pushing. Just promise me you won't shred the file."

Melanie stared at the file she'd been fingering throughout the conversation as if it were some sort of talisman that linked her to Richard. "Fine. I won't destroy the file." She stared hard at Becky. "And you won't call Jason."

"But—"

"No, buts," Melanie said firmly. "Let the man grovel for once. You know he will."

"Eventually," Becky agreed confidently. Her cheerful mood returned. "Before I land him, the man is going to have groveling down to a fine art."

"Now there's a goal." Melanie regarded Becky wistfully. "I wonder if Richard knows the first thing about groveling?" She thought of how goal oriented he claimed to be and sighed. "Doubtful," she concluded.

"Maybe he's trainable," Becky suggested.

Destiny had had a certain amount of luck teaching him manners, but she'd started at a relatively early age. Melanie had a hunch she was catching Richard far too late to change his ingrained habits.

Too bad, too, because more than once over the weekend, she thought he'd displayed amazing possibilities...and not one of them had anything at all to do with his candidacy for City Council.

She was still pondering that when the phone rang. Becky picked it up.

"Hart Consulting," she said cheerfully, then listened, her expression going from surprised to dismayed so quickly that Melanie's heart was thudding when Becky finally handed over the receiver.

Becky punched the hold button before Melanie could speak. "Prepare yourself. It's that columnist from the morning paper. He's asking about you and Richard."

"About the consulting?" Melanie asked hopefully.

Becky shook her head. "About the weekend you spent together. He seems to have details."

Oh, hell. This was a publicist's worst nightmare, even when she wasn't personally involved. Worse, it was too late to duck the call. Melanie sucked in a deep breath and prepared for some fancy tap dancing. She had to find out how much the reporter knew, or thought he knew.

"This is Melanie Hart," she said briskly.

"Pete Forsythe, Ms. Hart. How are you? We met at the heart association gala last month."

"Of course, I remember you, Mr. Forsythe. What can I do for you?"

"I'm looking for confirmation on something I heard this morning from an extremely reliable source."

"Oh?"

"It involves you and Carlton Industries CEO and chairman Richard Carlton."

"Really? I can't imagine where you'd hear anything linking the two of us in any way. I barely know Mr. Carlton."

"But you do know him," he persisted.

"We've met."

"Is there any truth to the rumor that the two of you are involved? That you spent this weekend with him at a family cottage at the beach?"

Melanie's laugh sounded forced, even to her. "Don't be ridiculous. As I said, I barely know the man. Sorry, Mr. Forsythe. I can't help you." She hung up before he could press her into saying something she'd regret, something that would send Richard into a blind rage.

"Is he going to print an item anyway?" Becky asked.

"More than likely."

"Are you going to warn Richard?"

Melanie considered it and decided it wouldn't help anything. She hadn't given anything away. Richard might be angry enough to call Pete Forsythe and protest the man's intrusion into his privacy, which would only add fuel to the fire. Better to let Forsythe think that there was no fire, that the rumor was off the mark. Maybe then, if he had even the tiniest shred of integrity, he'd have second thoughts about printing it.

"No," she told Becky. "Maybe without my confirmation, Forsythe will conclude that there's nothing to the gossip and drop it."

Becky promptly shook her head. "I think you're being blindly optimistic. This is too juicy. I'd certainly want to know if a powerful man like Carlton, who's thinking of running for office, was holed up in a cozy little getaway with a major PR consultant. That's hot stuff in this town. With what he has now, he can spin it a lot of different ways. An intimate rendezvous? A campaign strategy session that confirms Richard's intention to run for Council? Either way, it's news.''

Melanie couldn't deny that. She could only pray that Pete Forsythe was the kind of reporter who'd want confirmation from at least one of the participants before printing anything, before deciding on what angle to pursue. He hadn't gotten any sort of confirmation from her, and she doubted he'd risk going straight to Richard. Carlton Industries spent a lot of money in advertising, and Richard was a powerful man in the business community. Would Forsythe or his paper risk offending him for a titillating tidbit in tomorrow's paper? The story could still die, she told herself staunchly. Really.

Sure, she thought grimly, and pigs could fly.

Chapter Seven

"Why was one of Alexandria's most eligible bachelors huddling in a secret hideaway with a marketing expert last weekend?" Pete Forsythe's insider column in the Washington paper asked a few days later. "Could it be that Carlton Industries CEO Richard Carlton is finally getting ready for that long-rumored plunge into politics? Or was this *rendezvous* personal? He's not talking and neither is the woman, but we've confirmed that he was tucked away during last weekend's snowstorm with Melanie Hart, an up-and-coming star on the local marketing and public relations scene."

Richard tossed the newspaper in the trash where it belonged and buzzed his secretary. "Winifred, get Melanie Hart over here now!"

"Yes, sir."

Melanie must have been lurking in the lobby, because she was in his office in less than ten minutes. She looked good, too. Great, in fact, as if she'd prepared for just the right look to get him to pay more attention to her than this situation she'd created by blabbing their business all over town. If she was still trying to convince him to hire her, she'd gone about it all wrong. He was fit to be tied.

"I had a feeling I'd be hearing from you. I was already on my way over here," she told him, studying him worriedly. "I saw the paper this morning. How furious are you?"

"On a scale of one to ten, I'd say twelve thousand," he retorted. "I do not intend to play out my campaign intentions or my personal life in some damned gossip column. You ought to know that."

She stared at him a minute, apparently absorbing his barely disguised accusation, then said icily, "I do. I know it, not because I have a clue what goes on in that impossibly hard head of yours, but because it's a bad strategy. It diminishes you as a candidate to have people perceive that you're sneaking around with a woman for any reason whatsoever."

Richard was taken aback by her blunt response. What made her think she could get away with being some sort of victim? He scowled right back at her. "Then what the hell were you thinking?" There it was. He'd said it. Now let her dance around and try to avoid the obvious. Only the two of them knew about the weekend, and he'd never spoken to Forsythe.

"Me?" she said, radiating indignation. "I had nothing to do with this. This isn't exactly great for my reputation, either."

His frown deepened, but for an instant his fury wavered. She'd made the denial sound almost believ-able. His temper cooled marginally as he struggled to give her the benefit of the doubt. What she'd said made sense. He regarded her intently, wanting desperately to believe she hadn't betrayed him. "Then you're swearing to me that you did not plant that item?"

She gave him another one of those withering looks intended to make him feel like slime.

"Absolutely not," she swore.

Richard knew then that he owed her an apology, but he couldn't quite bring himself to utter it, not without asking a few more questions. "Did you speak to Forsythe?"

Her expression faltered at that. "Yes, but—"

Richard seized on the admission, not even waiting for her explanation. "Why the hell would you even take his call? I didn't. He never got past my secretary. No good can ever come from talking to a gossip columnist. You're a professional. You should know that."

"What I know is that sometimes a *reporter* can be an ally, if you know when to talk and what to say," she retorted. "Besides, I was already committed to taking the call before I knew why he was calling. As soon as I realized what he was after, I thought it would be wise to find out exactly what he'd heard. Once he started asking questions about you and me being at the cottage, I danced around the answers and hung up."

Richard sighed. She was making too damned much sense to be flat-out lying. "Then you never confirmed the story?"

She scowled at him. "Do I look that stupid?"

"Then who the hell was so reliable that Forsythe would print the story without confirmation from one of us? Someone in your office?"

"No. Becky would never do something like that."

"Not even in some misguided attempt to do you a favor?"

"Never."

"Who else knew you were down there?" he demanded, then stared at her stricken face as understanding dawned on both of them. He said it first. "Destiny, of course."

Even though she'd clearly been leaning in the same direction, Melanie looked genuinely shocked that he would accuse his aunt of betraying them. "Surely, she wouldn't do such a thing?"

Richard's laugh was forced. "Oh, yes, she would, especially if she thought planting that story in the paper would accomplish her goal."

"Do you know what her goal is? Because frankly, I'm a little confused."

"No, you're not. You've already confronted her about it. She wants us together," he said grimly. If he hadn't known it before, he did now. This was the act of a very determined matchmaker.

"You mean me working for you," Melanie replied, still trying for a positive spin.

"No, *together* together," he said impatiently. "A couple."

Melanie turned pale, and for the first time since entering his office, she sank onto a chair. "Are you sure?"

"Oh, yes. I know my aunt and she's all but admitted as much, though if she'd been half as good at skirting the truth with Forsythe as she was with me, we wouldn't be in this mess. That tells me she very deliberately spilled the beans.''

"This is crazy," Melanie said. "She can't just manipulate us into doing what she wants. We're two reasonable adults who are perfectly capable of making our own decisions, and we've decided that we're completely unsuited.'' She met his gaze. "Haven't we?''

"That was the way we left it this weekend," Richard agreed.

"Then all we need to do is tell her that.''

"I did.''

"And?''

He dragged the paper out of the trash and waved it in her direction. "This was her response. She's obviously not giving up.''

"She's your aunt. Do something.''

Richard gave her a rueful look. He'd never been any good at thwarting Destiny when she was on a mission. It was smarter to give in than to wait to be mowed down. Maybe Melanie would have a better tactic.

"Any suggestions?" he asked.

He waited as her expression turned thoughtful, then forlorn.

"None," she said finally. "You? You know her better than I do. Surely you can think of something to get her off this tangent.''

Short of strangling her, there weren't a lot of viable options, even fewer he could live with. It struck Richard that they were simply going to have to play this out. He felt only minimally guilty that he didn't feel nearly as bad about that as he probably should. Still, he managed a resigned air as he said grimly, ''Then we have absolutely no choice. We give her what she wants.''

Melanie stared. "Huh?"

He grinned. "I thought you were quicker to catch on to things.''

"Not this," she admitted. "This seems a little out there, like a publicity stunt that's doomed to failure.''

"It'll work. Trust me," Richard said, injecting a note of certainty into his voice.

"Let me be sure I have this straight," Melanie said, as if she were grappling with a Nobel Prize caliber physics theory. "You're suggesting that you and I pretend to be together to get Destiny to back off?''

Watching the flash of heat in Melanie's eyes, Richard began to warm to the idea. The part of himself he'd been struggling to ignore all weekend long was ecstatic about this new strategy, despite its obvious risks. In fact, he had no intention of looking too closely at the risks.

"That is exactly what I mean," he said, trying not to sound too eager.

Melanie looked doubtful, not disgusted. He took that as a good sign.

"Won't she be hard to convince?" she asked.

Richard considered his aunt's insightful nature. "Very hard," he agreed. In this case, that might work to his advantage. It would buy him some time to see if these odd feelings of his when he was around Melanie really meant anything. Since he'd never experienced anything quite like them before, he couldn't be sure.

"Then where are we going to draw the line?"

Richard studied the woman seated on the edge of her chair, bright patches of color in her otherwise pale cheeks. "We might have to be a little flexible on that."

Melanie shook her head. "I don't think so," she said adamantly. "Couldn't you just hire me, the way she asked you to? Wouldn't that satisfy her?"

"Sweetheart, I think it's fairly clear by now that that was just a smoke screen. Heaven knows why, but she won't be happy till we've walked down the aisle."

Horror registered on Melanie's face. "I am not marrying you."

"No kidding," he said, more than ready to agree with her on that. Not even he was prepared to carry this charade to that extreme, but a few weeks of getting close to Melanie and giving Destiny what she so clearly wanted held a certain undeniable appeal. "I think we can draw the line there. No marriage."

"No sleeping together, either," she added, giving him a hard stare. "I want to be clear about that, too."

"We might have to negotiate on that one," he said, feeling a whole lot better about things. Maybe he could turn this into a win-win situation instead of a disaster, after all. "So, Ms. Hart, you're hired."

She blinked in confusion. "As your new marketing person?"

"No. As my fiancée-to-be. No pay, but there will be a lot of perks."

"You want me to market myself to your aunt as your fiancée?" she asked, her expression incredulous.

"Fiancée-to-be," he corrected. "For starters."

"Whatever," Melanie said dismissively. "Isn't that a huge leap? She can't possibly think we're engaged or even about to be engaged. We've just barely met, and she knows that first meeting did not go well at all.''

''Ah, but last weekend,'' Richard said, affecting a tone of pure rapture.

''Oh, stuff a sock in it,'' Melanie said irritably. ''She won't buy an engagement this quickly. She's too smart for that. She might think I'm dumb enough to fall for you in ten seconds flat, but she's bound to know that you're not the type to fall in love at first sight. Heck, you've probably already told her that I'm not your type.''

He flushed at that. ''Doesn't matter. Destiny is a romantic at heart,'' Richard said. He'd never noticed that about his aunt before, but her meddling was giving him whole new insights into her personality quirks. ''She wants us together. If we go out a few times, let her catch us kissing from time to time, then say we're engaged in a week or two, trust me, she won't look any deeper.''

''This is crazy,'' Melanie said again. ''There has to be some other way besides lying to your aunt.''

He gazed into her eyes. ''Let me be clear about something. This isn't just about my aunt, Melanie. After Forsythe's column, we have to convince the entire world that you and I fell madly, passionately in love and can't bear to be apart.'' He gave her a wry look. ''It was the last thing either of us expected, of course.''

''Of course,'' Melanie said with a decidedly sarcastic edge to her voice.

He picked up his pen and made a note to start arranging some family get-togethers, then glanced at Melanie, who looked as if she might be about to explode. ''We're all set, then, right?''

She stared at him incredulously. "No, we are not all set. I hate this."

"I'm not crazy about it myself, but I can't see any other solution. We have to make it real. People will forgive a prospective candidate a lot if there's love involved. They're not so forgiving of sleazy affairs."

She was shaking her head. "I don't think so."

"Do you have a better plan to extricate us from this?"

She regarded him with an undeniable hint of desperation in her eyes, then sighed. "No."

He took pity on her. "I'll let you stage a bang-up scene when you dump me," he offered, fairly sure that a chance to humiliate him would appeal to her baser instincts. It might make her feel better about letting him back her into this corner, which, frankly, was more fun than he'd had in ages. Maybe he did owe Destiny, after all.

As he'd predicted, Melanie looked intrigued by the prospect of getting even. "In public?" she bargained.

"Won't be any fun if it's not in public," he agreed, willing to endure the humiliation if it gave him a few weeks to woo Melanie into his bed. That was his short-term—his *only*—goal. He had to remember that. Getting even with Destiny, getting public perception back on his side, those were purely a bonus. Happily-ever-after was out of the question. He didn't believe in it. Or, perhaps more accurately, he didn't trust himself to want it.

"How long do we carry out the charade before I get to dump you?" Melanie inquired.

Richard gave the question the serious consideration it deserved. Melanie had a right to know how much of a commitment she was making. "For as long as it takes to get Destiny off our backs and make it believable for everybody else.''

"A month?'' she asked hopefully.

"She'll never buy it.''

"Two?''

"How about six and we'll see where we stand?'' He gazed deeper into her eyes. "There's no one in your life who'll object, is there?''

"Sadly, no,'' she said. "Believe me, I'd love to have an excuse to get out of this.'' She gave him a knowing look. "But you knew that, didn't you?''

"I was reasonably confident that you wouldn't have traipsed after me to that cottage if there had been an important man in your life.''

Her gaze narrowed. "I came down there on business. Even if there was a man in my life, he wouldn't have the right to object to me taking a business trip.''

"He wouldn't have left you down there, snowbound with me, though, would he? Not if he had an ounce of sense. He'd have been there to rescue you by dawn on Saturday.''

"Nothing happened that needed to be explained or forgiven,'' she retorted, eyes flashing.

Richard gave her an innocent look. "Really? Here I thought that was when we fell in love.''

Melanie groaned. "Do you have any idea how much I hate this?'' she asked again.

"You've mentioned that,'' he admitted. "But you're going to go along with it, aren't you?''

For a minute it almost looked as if she might balk, but then she finally nodded.

At her acquiescence—albeit reluctant—Richard felt the oddest sensation in his chest. It felt a whole lot like relief. Or maybe elation. He couldn't be sure. It wasn't a sensation he'd ever experienced before. That was happening a lot lately.

Melanie's head was spinning. She had just agreed to pose as Richard's almost-fiancée for the foreseeable future. There was no question in her mind that this was going to be a role she could handle by making an occasional appearance by his side in public. He was going to insist that she give it her all to make it believable, at least to one person. Unfortunately for both of them, there was also little doubt that Destiny was going to be a hard sell.

So why try? Melanie asked herself that repeatedly on the drive back to her office. Why had she agreed to this? Because she'd felt guilty over that stupid item in the morning paper? That hadn't been her doing. Because she had some insane idea that this was the only way to get Destiny to leave them alone? Richard might be convinced of that, but she wasn't. Not entirely, anyway. So, what was the real reason?

Because some teeny-tiny, totally insane part of her wanted it to be true. Even as the thought crept in, she was shouting no-no-no to herself as emphatically as she possibly could. The noise was so loud in her head, she barely heard the cell phone when it rang. Relieved to have an excuse to turn off her own chaotic thoughts, she punched the button on the dash that put the call on speaker.

"Yes," she barked.

"Show time," Richard said.

"What?"

"We're having dinner with Destiny tonight."

"How did that happen? I just left you ten minutes

ago. Word couldn't have gotten back to her that quickly.''

"I called," he told her without the least hint of regret. "Preemptive strike."

"Are you crazy? I haven't even gotten used to the idea. I'll bungle this."

"Just follow my lead. I'll pick you up at seven. Wear something glamorous. Destiny likes to dress for dinner."

He hung up before Melanie could get a vehement objection to cross her lips. What was he thinking? Maybe he figured it was like swimming—better to toss her into the deep end to test her mettle than to wishy-wash around in the kiddie pool for weeks.

If she was going to do this, she needed help. She punched speed dial for her office.

"Becky, I need you to meet me at Chez Deux in ten minutes."

"Why?"

"I'll explain when I see you. Dig a charge card out of the office safe."

"Which one?"

"The one with the biggest credit line," she said grimly.

Under other circumstances, Melanie loved to shop. Not that she was ever extravagant, not with a comparatively new business to run, but she loved clothes. Chez Deux with its line of secondhand designer clothes suited her budget and her desire to dress for success. Normally, however, she was picking suits off the rack, not evening wear. If she forgot the reason for this shopping expedition, it could still be fun.

She found a parking space a block away, then

trudged carefully over the cobblestone sidewalks to avoid the occasional patch of leftover ice.

"Hey, Jasmin," she greeted the owner when she got to the classy little shop, which accepted consignments from many of Washington's best-dressed women.

"Ms. Hart, how nice to see you," Jasmin Trudeau said. "We have some lovely new suits in your size."

"Not today. Today I'm looking for something a little fancier, for a formal dinner party."

The petite woman's eyes lit up. "Then the rumors are true, *n'est-ce pas?* I saw the story in this morning's paper."

Melanie wanted to deny it, but Jasmin was one of the city's biggest sources of socialite gossip. If Melanie declared the story entirely untrue, it would be all over town by evening, pretty much defeating this charade she and Richard were embarking on.

"I am having dinner with Mr. Carlton tonight," she admitted, leaving it at that.

"Then you must look your very best. I have just the thing," Jasmin said. "It came in only yesterday. I have not even put it on the rack yet. One moment and I will get it for you."

Becky arrived just then, looking harried and curious. "What on earth is going on?"

"I'm buying a dress," Melanie said.

"I got that much. What kind of dress and why?"

"A fancy, expensive dress. I need the fortification."

Becky stared at her blankly. "Huh?"

"Let me get this over with, and I'll take you out for a long leisurely lunch, so you can tell me I haven't completely lost my mind."

Becky hid her disappointment and silenced her questions as Jasmin reappeared with a strapless dress in bronze satin.

"This dress was made for you," Jasmin said. "Do not look at the price. If it looks as fabulous on you as I think it will, you will not care what it costs."

Melanie was already itching to slip the rich fabric over her head. She took it gingerly and headed for a dressing room. In seconds she had stripped off her clothes and slipped the dress on. Only when she had it zipped up did she risk a look in the mirror. "Oh, my," she whispered. She felt like Cinderella after she was outfitted for the ball, not quite like herself…or maybe more like herself than she'd ever been before.

"Hey, stop hiding in there and get out here," Becky commanded. "Jasmin and I are dying of curiosity."

Melanie stepped out of the dressing room. Both women's eyes widened.

"You look *fabulous,*" Becky said.

"Mr. Carlton will not be able to resist you," Jasmin added, as if that were a bonus.

Before Becky could ask what the heck the other woman meant by that, Melanie said quickly, "I'll take the dress." Jasmin had been right. She didn't care what it cost. Whatever it was, it was a small price to pay to walk into Destiny's house tonight feeling confident as she and Richard launched this charade. And she could always have it cleaned and bring it right back here on consignment to recoup some of the cost, though something told her she would never give it up.

Once she'd added an outrageously expensive jeweled purse, she signed the credit-card slip without giving it a second glance. Maybe if her accountant turned a blind eye, she could figure out some way to turn this into a business expense.

When the transaction was completed, she took her purchases to her car. Becky trailed along behind, muttering a barrage of questions that Melanie determinedly ignored. Only when her packages were stowed away and they were seated in a nearby restaurant with coffee on the table and salads on the way did she finally look her friend in the eye.

"You have to promise that you will never breathe one single word of what I am about to tell you," she told Becky. "Not one word. Not to your own mother. Not even to a lawyer, a priest or anyone else sworn to uphold your confidentiality."

Becky solemnly crossed her heart. "My God, Melanie, what have you done? You didn't kill Pete Forsythe, did you?"

"No, though in retrospect, that might have made more sense than this."

"Then you saw Richard?"

"Oh, yeah."

"And he was furious?"

"About as furious as I anticipated when I told you I was going over there this morning to try to head off an explosion."

"Did you figure out who leaked the story?"

"He's convinced it was Destiny."

"His own aunt?" Becky said incredulously.

Melanie nodded. "It gets worse. He's also convinced she won't be happy until he and I really are involved, so he's decided we need to pretend that we are."

Becky blinked hard, then her expression slowly

changed to comprehension. "That explains the dress."

"Yep. We're having dinner with Destiny tonight."

"You actually went along with this?" Becky asked, sounding incredulous. "You're going to lie to a woman who befriended you?"

"A woman who befriended me with ulterior motives," Melanie corrected. "It's a fine point, but an important one."

"Oh, brother."

Melanie met Becky's gaze. "Am I crazy?"

"Probably."

"Is there any way this can not go horribly wrong?"

"Not that I can see," Becky said, sounding surprisingly cheerful.

"Why are you suddenly finding this so amusing?" Melanie demanded.

"Because you are both so obviously delusional."

"Why do you say that?"

"Richard thinks he's doing this to get even with his aunt, am I right?"

"Yes."

"And you're doing it out of some misguided sense of guilt, correct?"

Melanie nodded.

"Ha!"

Melanie frowned at her. "What is that supposed to mean?"

"You're both doing it because you want it to be true. He wants to be involved with you. You want to be involved with him. Neither of you is willing to be honest about it." Becky took a little bow. "You're welcome."

Melanie gave her a sour look. "I didn't thank you."

"You should have," Becky told her. "It's the most honest thing that's been said at this table since we sat down."

Melanie opened her mouth to deny it, then snapped her mouth shut again. There had been enough lies and half-truths and deceptions floating around today.

"This really is going to be a disaster, isn't it?" she said eventually.

Becky nodded without hesitation. "That would be my assessment, yes." She gave Melanie a sympathetic look. "You could still fix it."

"How?"

"Make it real."

"No. Neither of us wants that."

Becky rolled her eyes.

"Okay, Richard doesn't want that and I'm almost certain I don't, either. We hardly know each other, but I do know he's a man who's not in touch with his feelings, he's still a potential client and he's stodgy. Those are all things that make him bad for me."

"You're hopeless," Becky said. "At least I'm in touch with my feelings." She grinned. "Jason is groveling, by the way. It's lovely."

"Good for Jason." She gave Becky a defeated look. "How am I going to fix this?"

"You're obviously not, at least not the mature, intelligent way, since you won't acknowledge the truth. That means you have to go with the flow."

"I'm lousy at going with the flow," Melanie reminded her.

Becky grinned. "I know. That's what's going to make this so much fun to watch."

Chapter Eight

Richard rarely questioned his decisions once he'd made them. Having second thoughts was the mark of a man who didn't know his own mind, and he prided himself on his clarity of thought. Or he had until today.

Now that the dust had settled over that ridiculous rumor in the morning paper, he realized that talk would have died down in a day or two with no real harm done. That was how he should have handled it, simply let it go away of its own accord. Instead, he'd turned it into this big charade that was going to turn his life inside out for weeks, maybe even months to come.

He'd gotten caught up in the heat of the moment. He'd wanted to pay Destiny back for her meddling. He'd wanted to go on spending time with Melanie without having her underfoot professionally. That was both unfair and insulting. He was surprised she'd gone along with it. She should have told him to take a hike. He couldn't help wondering why she hadn't. Maybe she was suffering from the same momentary lunacy that was affecting him.

Now he'd gone and compounded his mistake by deciding to drag a perfectly nice woman into his aunt's web of intrigue, when he should have been doing everything in his power to keep the two of them as far apart as humanly possible. His head pounded just thinking about what dinner was going to be like.

Hoping for backup, he picked up the phone and called his brother Mack.

"Well, well, if it isn't the newly proclaimed Romeo of the family," Mack taunted when he heard Richard's voice.

"Go to hell."

Mack laughed. Mack was used to having his name bandied all over town, linked with a different socialite each time. Richard was not.

"As soon as you're through enjoying this, I have a favor to ask," Richard announced grimly.

"Anything," Mack said, instantly sober. "You know that. Should I go over to the paper and put the fear of God into Pete Forsythe? I've been dying to have a legitimate excuse for a long time now. Unfortunately, most of what he reports about me is true. The man's a menace to the privacy of all bachelors."

"Not worth getting your knuckles roughed up," Richard said.

"I wasn't planning to resort to brute force, despite my reputation from the football field," Mack said, sounding wounded that Richard thought so little of him. "I can be intimidating in other ways."

Richard chuckled despite his lousy mood. "Believe me, I am aware of that. Actually, though, I was hoping you'd back me up at Destiny's tonight. Intimidate her a little."

"Oh, no," Mack said. "She is obviously on one of her matchmaking tears. When she gets this way, I prefer flying under her radar."

"Believe me, she's going to be too busy focusing on me tonight to worry about you," Richard told him. "I'm taking Melanie Hart to dinner."

Mack whistled. "Oh, brother, you are living dangerously, aren't you? Or is something really going on between you and this woman?"

"There is nothing going on," Richard assured him. "But I want Destiny to think otherwise."

"Why the hell would you want that?"

"I'm hoping Destiny will back off if she's convinced I'm doing exactly what she wanted," Richard explained. "And if you tell another living, breathing soul I said that, I'll make sure that Destiny tries to hook you up with the most avaricious, impossible female in this entire region. Believe me, I know some of the worst. I'll give her a list of candidates guaranteed to make your life miserable."

"Speaking of intimidation," Mack said quietly, "you're not bad at it yourself."

"Thank you. Will you be there?"

"How could I possibly refuse such a gracious invitation to dine with my family?" Mack said with a sarcastic bite to his voice. "Are you calling Ben?"

"No, I think you'll do for now."

"But baby brother might enjoy this," Mack objected. "He's never seen you on the ropes before.

We've always thought you were invincible, afraid of nothing.''

"Very amusing. Besides, Ben doesn't enjoy anything that means he has to leave his farm in Middleburg and stop brooding for an entire evening. On top of that, he's too honest for conspiracies.''

"And I'm not?'' Mack inquired with a touch of indignation.

"Not even close. You thrive on them. That's why you're so good at using sneaky, clever tactics to lure the best, most unavailable football talent to your team,'' Richard said. "Seven-thirty, okay?''

"Despite the number of times you've insulted me in this conversation, I'll be there,'' Mack promised. "Hope I can keep a straight face.''

"Consider the alternative,'' Richard told him grimly.

After he'd hung up, he kept staring at the phone. He loved his brother. He knew Mack would go to the mat for him or for Ben, but an actor? No way. It was entirely possible he'd just made his second-worst mistake of the day. Apparently he was on a real roll.

Melanie had anticipated a barrage of last-minute instructions from Richard on the drive to his aunt's. Instead, beyond an approving once-over and a friendly-enough greeting when he'd picked her up, he'd remained stoically silent. It was getting on her nerves.

"Don't you think maybe we should go over our plan?'' she asked finally.

He glanced at her then, the line of his jaw hard. "You think I actually have a plan?''

"I was hoping for one, yes. You have a reputation

for being very organized, for leaving nothing to chance.''

His laugh sounded forced. ''So I do. Apparently it's my day for doing the unexpected.''

''So there really is no plan,'' she surmised, feeling suddenly queasy. She could wing it with a mob of reporters, but this? This was definitely not a situation in which she should be flying by the seat of her pants. Surely, Richard should understand that. She cleared her throat. ''Um, don't you think maybe we should stop for a second and get a few things straight?''

This time when he glanced her way, his gaze lingered. ''You really are nervous, aren't you?''

''Well, duh! What do you think? I am about to face a woman I like and respect and pretend that I'm falling for her favorite nephew. I anticipate a lot of questions. Don't you?''

''I'm not her favorite. Destiny doesn't have favorites. She's always been very clear about that.'' He grinned. ''Mack and I both know it's Ben. He has her artistic talent, if not her quixotic nature. Mack loves sports, which she doesn't get at all, and she thinks I'm stuffy.''

''Okay, whatever,'' Melanie retorted, not sounding remotely sympathetic. ''The point is that we're lying to her and we don't have our stories straight.''

''Mack will be there. He'll be a good buffer. He's quite a talker. We may not have to say much.''

She stared at him in shock. ''Oh, goody. I get to lie to your brother, too.''

''No, he gets that this is a sham.''

Her stomach dropped. ''And that's better? You expect him to lie, too?''

''No, I expect him to take some of the heat off of

us. Mack has a way of stirring Destiny up. You'll see. It's actually rather fascinating to watch.''

"Why on earth would your brother agree to be a party to this?'' When Richard didn't answer, she reached her own conclusion. ''You bribed him, didn't you? Or threatened him?''

He frowned at that. ''Only in a brotherly kind of way,'' he insisted as if that made it so much better. ''I told him if he didn't help, I could see to it that Destiny turned her misguided attentions on him.''

"And?'' She knew there was more. There had to be.

"I might have hinted that I could influence the choice she made and that the woman might not be to Mack's liking.''

Melanie regarded him with dismay. ''Do you hate your brother that much?''

"Of course not,'' he said, staring at her as if she were crazy.

"Then why would you even suggest such a thing, given how thrilled you are to be in this particular mess?''

"Misery loves company,'' he suggested glibly.

Melanie merely buried her face in her hands and prayed for a quick end to the entire evening.

Melanie didn't seem happy, which made two of them, Richard concluded as he pulled into the three-car garage at what had once been his home. The brick town house in Old Town Alexandria combined two old homes into one gracious enough for entertaining and big enough for the large family his parents had anticipated. It had black shutters and brass trim and an occasional tendril of ivy that had escaped the gardener's attention climbing up the pink brick.

In recent years Destiny had remained there as first he, then Mack and then Ben had moved into homes of their own. For the first time he considered that maybe his aunt was doing all this matchmaking craziness because she was lonely. Too bad he couldn't fix *her* up. Maybe that would end this madness.

Unfortunately, even the thought of trying to turn the tables and hook Destiny up with some man made him smile. His aunt would not be amused. Her personal life was not a topic he or his brothers approached without serious trepidation. She always cut them off before they could complete their first query. He would have thought that a woman so tight-lipped about her own intimate secrets would be more careful about sticking her nose into his.

As he got out of the car, he took a second look at the flashy red convertible she'd bought recently and shook his head. It was entirely possible she was going through some sort of midlife crisis, though come to think of it the convertible suited her personality a whole lot better than the minivans she'd driven when they were boys.

"Your aunt loves that car," Melanie noted. "I was with her when she bought it."

He regarded her with surprise. "You were?" Then he recalled the rest of the story. "You were the woman who ran into her car that day and totaled it? That's how the two of you met?"

Melanie winced. "I thought you knew."

He shook his head. "This just gets better and better. I thought she'd met you on some committee or other. I figured she'd seen you doing PR and recommended you because of that. Instead, she met you in a traffic accident.'' He rubbed his now-throbbing temples. ''It all makes perfect sense.''

Melanie blinked. ''It does?''

''Sure. She really has gone 'round the bend. Instead of going in there and trying to convince her we're involved, I ought to be trying to convince her to see a shrink.''

Melanie glowered at him. ''Do you know how insulting that is? To both of us, in fact.''

He heard the anger in her voice and knew this whole evening was within a nanosecond of blowing up in his face. He forced a smile. ''Sorry. My head hurts.''

''It should. Given the size of your ego, I'm shocked it hasn't exploded.''

He grinned. ''Nice one. Are we even yet?''

''Not by a long shot,'' she said, sweeping past him. ''Let's get this over with.''

''By all means,'' he said as he shut the garage door behind them, then led her toward the front entrance. The door was open and light was spilling out onto the street. ''Mack must have beat us here.''

Sure enough, his brother was in the foyer and his aunt was chiding him for not wearing an overcoat.

''Destiny, I parked less than ten yards away from the front door,'' Mack said, defending himself as if he were twelve, rather than a grown man. ''It's not that cold out. Besides, I have all this muscle.''

''Between your ears, mainly,'' Destiny said, cuffing him gently. ''I really thought I raised you with more sense.''

''You did,'' Mack said, kissing her. ''You made me the man I am today, no question about it.'' He grinned at Richard over her head. "Look who's here. Big brother and his new girl."

Destiny whirled around, a smile spreading across her face. She rushed forward and embraced Melanie with genuine affection. "Darling, I'm delighted you're here. Don't mind Mack. Too many sacks on the football field knocked out most of his manners."

"I had fewer sacks than any quarterback in the National Football League," he countered. "I'm very quick on my feet."

"You were," Richard agreed. "Unfortunately it only took one sack to wipe out your knee and destroy your career." He pulled Melanie forward. "Melanie Hart, this is Mighty Mack Carlton, ex-football hero who is still reliving his glory days on the field every chance he gets, especially if it'll help him score with some female."

"A fine way to talk about your brother," Destiny scolded, linking her arm through Melanie's. "Pay no attention to either one of them. They're barbarians. I'd disown them, if it weren't too late."

Mack grinned at her. "Destiny, there's still time to change your will. You can leave all your money to your cats. Sad, lonely spinsters do that all the time."

Destiny scowled. "I'm neither sad nor lonely, and I don't own any cats."

"Then get some," Mack advised. "You're going to need the company when you run all of us off."

Destiny turned to Melanie. "See what I have to put up with? Consider this fair warning. If you continue going out with my nephew, you'll find that we're a tough crowd to love."

Richard wondered if that was an out he could use.

While he was pondering the possibilities, Mack jumped in.

"Listen to her," Mack advised Melanie. "Get out while you can."

Melanie glanced toward Richard, her expression hopeful. She clearly wanted him to give her some signal whether this was indeed the moment she should cut and run for the nearest exit.

Richard winked at her. "Have a drink instead. It'll make the rest of the evening more bearable."

Between Mack's teasing and Destiny's quick retorts, Richard and Melanie remained safely off the hot seat at least through the appetizers. But when Destiny led the way into the dining room and seated Melanie right next to her and him at the opposite end of the long table, Richard knew the gloves were about to come off. There was nothing he could do to protect Melanie now. He hoped she really was quick on her feet with diplomatic evasions.

"Darling," Destiny said to Melanie over the soup, "have I told you how delighted I am that Richard invited you to join us this evening?"

Melanie managed a weak smile. "Thank you."

"The two of you have so much in common," Destiny continued in the same slick tone she might use if she were about to sell her a used car.

"We do?" Melanie said skeptically.

"Of course you do. Or perhaps I should say that your talents and interests are complementary. You have exactly what Richard needs to fulfill his destiny."

Richard choked on a sip of water. He hadn't expected his aunt to go quite this far. It was beginning to look as if she wanted to seal this deal tonight. He wouldn't be surprised to see her whip out an engagement ring.

"I'm sure Melanie appreciates the intended compliment, but I think you're embarrassing her," Richard said, giving Melanie a bolstering smile. "Mack, why don't you tell us about the team's chances in the play-offs?"

Destiny cut Mack off before he could utter the first word. "There will be no talk of football over dinner," she said firmly.

Mack rolled his eyes. "You say that as if it involves talk of blood and gore."

Richard sat back happily, his mission accomplished. He knew from past experience that Mack and Destiny could spend hours debating whether football was a real sport or simply some macho excuse for a bunch of men to pummel each other senseless. Only the mention of boxing set her off more.

To his shock, Destiny waved off the comment. "I will not be drawn into this discussion tonight." She frowned at Richard. "Don't think I don't see what you're up to."

"Me?" Richard asked innocently. "What did I do?"

"You're trying to keep me from asking Melanie too many personal questions. You seem to have forgotten that I knew her before you did."

"Believe me, I have not forgotten that," Richard said grimly. "Not for an instant."

"Did she tell you about her sisters?"

"Yes."

"You know that she graduated from college magna cum laude?"

"I did not," Richard admitted. "Are you planning to trot out her résumé over the fish course?"

Destiny gave him a look that might have terrified him a few years back. Now he knew there was no real anger behind it. It was simply an intimidating tactic she'd found handy. He grinned at her. "Just thought I'd ask."

"Well, excuse me for trying to get it through your thick skull that she's very talented," Destiny said. "Talk to him, Mack. Tell him he's cutting off his nose to spite his face by trying to defy me."

Mack bit back a grin. "I think he heard you, Destiny."

Richard gave his aunt a bland look. "So if I were to hire Melanie right here, right now, you'd be happy?"

"That's all I ever wanted," Destiny said, her face the picture of innocence.

Richard shrugged, then turned to Melanie, who was listening to the exchange with an increasingly bemused expression. "You're hired."

She stared at him. "Really?"

"Really," he confirmed, then glanced at his aunt. "Satisfied?"

"I think you've made a very wise decision," she said happily. "That means the two of you will be working very closely together. Melanie, dear, would you like to move in here?"

Melanie choked on a sip of water. "Excuse me?"

"I thought it might be more convenient," Destiny said blithely.

"I have my own place."

"Not even two miles from here," Richard said, amused by his aunt's blatant attempt to maintain complete control over her protégé. "The only thing more convenient would be for her to move in with me."

Destiny's expression immediately brightened. "Perhaps until the election—"

"Absolutely not," Melanie said before Richard could gather his wits after the audacious suggestion. "I really don't need that much access to my clients, believe me. Sometimes a little distance is best for all concerned."

"Oh, I can't imagine that's true," Destiny said. "The more you know, the better prepared you'll be to represent Richard."

Melanie forced an insincere smile. "Something tells me I'm going to have plenty of inside information."

Destiny made no attempt to hide her disappointment. "Well, if you think that's best, dear. After all you are the expert. I'll certainly help all I can. Mack?"

Mack nodded, fighting a grin. "Believe me, I'll be Johnny-on-the-spot, whenever Melanie needs anything."

Richard didn't like the gleam in his brother's eye when he spoke. He gave him a warning scowl. "I think maybe it'll be best if Melanie and I work out my marketing strategy on our own with no outside interference. Too many cooks have a way of muddying the waters."

"I think they spoil the broth," Mack corrected, laughing. "But it's your call, big brother. If you want to keep Melanie all to yourself, I'm sure Destiny and I will respect your wishes, won't we, Destiny?"

Destiny could not be put off so easily. "If I have

suggestions from time to time, I'm sure Richard and Melanie will welcome them.''

"As if we could stop them," Richard muttered.

"Of course we'll welcome them," Melanie said, sounding more cheerful than she had at any time since their arrival. "I think this is going to turn out to be a match made in heaven."

Richard winced as his aunt beamed.

"I couldn't have said it better myself," Destiny said.

Mack choked back a laugh, then focused on his salmon. Richard looked around the table at the people who were apparently determined to drive him insane and sighed. This evening had not gone according to his roughly conceived plan. Not even close.

"I thought it went really well," Melanie said as they were driving home.

Richard's grim demeanor suggested he didn't agree.

"Okay, you may as well say it," she said. "You hate this, don't you?"

"Hate it?" he echoed. "I went in there with the upper hand. I came out like a man on the ropes."

"At least we're not engaged," Melanie said, determined to see the positives. "We're not even faking an engagement."

"Not yet," Richard said. "If you think that issue's off the table, you really are naive."

"Not off the table," she said defensively. "But we bought ourselves some time. Once Destiny gets all caught up in your campaign—"

"I do not want my aunt in the middle of my campaign," he said fiercely.

"Why on earth not? She's savvy. She knows people."

"She's sneaky, and I don't like the people she knows."

Melanie stared at him. "Don't you know the same people?"

"Yes, which is why I want no part of them," he said flatly. "Weren't you the one who kept stressing that I need to broaden my constituency?"

"Yes, but you also need money to run an effective campaign."

"I have money."

She stared at him incredulously. "You're going to spend your own money?"

"I have it," he repeated. "And that way I won't be beholden to a single special interest. That ought to make you happy."

"It makes me delirious," she said. "But are you sure it's wise? This is the time to start putting together the kind of powerful backing you'll need down the road."

"For?"

"A run for governor, for the Senate, whatever. I imagine this is just the start of your political aspirations. You can't finance all those campaigns out of your own pocket."

"Who knows, maybe after this I'll hate being a politician so much, I'll never run for anything again. We'll just have to wait and see," he said. "In the meantime, I don't want money from a bunch of people who'll think it's going to buy them access or favors."

Melanie was stunned, but it gave her an incredible angle to pursue once Richard had officially announced his intention to run. The public would eat it up.

"Let's get back to Destiny," he said. "Watch her, Melanie."

"Please, she's just trying to be helpful."

"There's helpful and then there's Destiny's version of help. I've seen her decline to chair a dozen different fund-raisers, but guess who makes all the critical decisions?"

"Your aunt," Melanie surmised, easily able to conceive of Destiny not staying behind the scenes.

"It won't be any different with my campaign."

"Let her make all the suggestions she wants to. We don't have to use a single one. We just have to listen," Melanie reminded him.

"No one will break our kneecaps if we don't," he agreed. "But there are other forms of coercion." He glanced over at her. "Want me to tell you what her first suggestion is going to be?"

Melanie was willing to play along. "Sure."

"She's going to ask you if you don't think I'd be a much stronger candidate if I were married," he said. "It's known as planting the seed. Destiny does love to dabble in her garden. She views me as one more plant she has to successfully nurture."

"But I don't think you have to be married to be successful, not that being a family man couldn't add another element to your image," Melanie said.

Richard gave her a triumphant look. "There you go. You just gave her the precise opening she'd need."

Melanie stared at him blankly. "I did?"

"Sure. I'm a good candidate now, but put a wife by my side and I'd be even better. Guess who the wife's supposed to be? You're here. You're handy. And we obviously get along well, don't you agree?'' he asked mockingly.

Melanie hated the fact that he was actually making sense. She could see Destiny happily traipsing down this path. Her high spirits were sinking fast. ''Like it or not, we're going to wind up engaged, aren't we?''

Richard nodded, his expression grim. ''It's only a matter of time.''

Melanie sank back against the rich leather of the seat and swallowed a sigh. She'd just landed the job of a lifetime, and it came with so many strings she was going to wind up hog-tied.

Chapter Nine

Richard tried to concentrate on the fax from his European division chairman explaining why profits were down and an intended acquisition had fallen through. Nothing in the report made a bit of sense, but maybe that was because Melanie's image kept swimming in front of him, making the words hard to read. The woman was driving him crazy, and she hadn't even been on his payroll for twenty-four hours yet.

Not that the fault was entirely hers. He was the one who'd been manipulated into making her a part of his everyday world. He'd been expecting her to turn up at the crack of dawn, but so far there had been no sign of her. Maybe—if the gods who protected fools were feeling very kindly—she'd decided against accepting the job coordinating his campaign PR. Maybe she possessed more sense than he did.

"You look a little wiped out, my friend," Mack

said, making a rare appearance in Richard's office at what was for Mack the ungodly hour of seven in the morning.

Richard stared at his brother. "What brings you by? I thought you preferred not to set foot in here out of fear that I might lock you into an office and put you to work for the family company."

"I think we established what a bad idea that would be a long time ago. I know football. I don't give a rat's behind about making widgets, or running restaurants or whatever else all those mysterious divisions do. I was lousy at Monopoly, if you remember. I kept selling my hotels and the land they sat on dirt cheap."

Richard gave his brother a wry look. "Frankly, I don't remember you ever sitting still long enough to play board games."

"There were a few rainy days when Destiny wouldn't let me outside to play football," Mack said. "You always whipped my butt, which did not bode well for my future at Carlton Industries. I may not be the business whiz you are, but even I could read the handwriting on that wall."

Richard regarded him with surprise. "You steered clear of the company because I beat you at Monopoly?"

"No, I steered clear because you love it and I don't, the same way Destiny left it behind for our father. This business ought to be run by someone who lives and breathes it. You do. Ben and I don't. Simple as that."

"Okay, if you're not here to stake a belated claim on a corner office, why are you here?"

"To do a postmortem on last night, of course," Mack said with a broad grin. "How are things going for you and your new campaign advisor? I'll bet that was a twist you never expected when you set up that dinner at Destiny's last night.''

''I am not up for that conversation at this hour of the morning,'' Richard said, unwilling to admit how deftly he'd been maneuvered into making that decision. ''I'll see Melanie later, establish some ground rules and we'll be okay.''

''Will that be before or after you ask her out on another fake date?'' Mack wondered aloud. ''Or has the grand charade been scrapped?''

Richard's gaze narrowed. ''Did Destiny put you up to coming in here this morning just to harangue me?''

''Nope. I'm here on my own,'' Mack insisted. ''I haven't had this much entertainment in weeks, not since some of the guys and I stopped watching *The Young and the Restless* during lunch in my office. Your plot's better, by the way. I can hardly wait to see how it turns out.''

Richard groaned. ''Keep it up, Mack. You're walking on thin ice.''

Mack grinned, evidently undaunted by Richard's increasingly sour mood. ''I liked her,'' he said. ''In case you're interested.''

''What's not to like?'' Richard conceded. ''Melanie's attractive, bright. And she has a good sense of humor. She must if she's willing to put up with all this craziness.''

''Plus she's kind to old ladies,'' Mack said with a straight face.

Richard chuckled in spite of himself. ''I'd like to be around when you suggest to Destiny that she's old.''

Mack winced. "A slip of the tongue, I assure you. Destiny is ageless."

"She is, isn't she?" Richard said with some regret. "Otherwise I could pretend that this is all about senility and ignore her."

"I think we can agree that our aunt is crazy like a fox." Mack's expression sobered. "Maybe you should pay attention to her, Richard. Seems to me you could do a whole lot worse than having Melanie in your life in whatever capacity turns out to fit best."

"Have you forgotten? She *is* in my life," Richard said, barely containing a sigh. "I'm having them clear out a little office right down the hall so she'll have a base right here in the building. With any luck, she'll never use it."

"Not what I meant, and you know it."

"Give it up, Mack. I have enough to contend with having Destiny sneaking around behind my back meddling. Don't you get any ideas."

"Hey, bro, I'm right out in the open." Mack's expression turned serious. "Listen to me. I think you're making a mistake if you don't give the woman a chance instead of playing games just to pacify Destiny. Go out on a real date with Melanie. Get to know her. Let your defenses down for once in your stodgy life."

"Now I'm stodgy?"

"You've always been stodgy. It's the natural by-product of deciding you had to be mature and responsible at the age of twelve, after Dad and Mom died. Thank God, Ben and I had you. Otherwise, we might have matured before our times as well."

"Whatever," Richard said, tired of the discussion. It was hitting uncomfortably close to the truth. Even with Destiny on the scene back then, he'd felt like he had to take charge, manage things to keep them from spinning any further out of control. One minute he'd been a normal kid, the next he'd been twelve-going-on-thirty.

"Of course," Mack said a little too casually, "if you're really not interested in anything personal with Melanie, I might be."

That damn vein in Richard's head started throbbing again. He wondered if it was a precursor to the stroke he was likely to have before all of this insanity ended. "Stay away from her," he said tightly. "No matter what I do or don't do, you stay the hell away from her."

Mack stood up, looking exceptionally pleased with himself. "Thought so," he gloated.

Richard glowered at him. "What does that mean?"

"You're the one with the agile mind," Mack said. "Think about it."

He sauntered out of the office whistling, leaving Richard to wrestle with the riddle his brother had left behind. Not that the answer was all that difficult to unravel. He just didn't want to see it.

Melanie passed Mack in the hallway as she was heading for Richard's office. He greeted her with a knowing grin she couldn't quite interpret.

"Good morning," she said cautiously. "Have you seen Richard?"

"In his office," Mack said. "You might want to give him a couple of minutes before you go in there."

"Is he in a meeting?"

"Nope, just wrestling with his inner demons," Mack said, a note of satisfaction in his voice.

"What just happened in there, or dare I ask?" she asked, wondering if Mack took as much pleasure in stirring up Richard as he did in rattling Destiny.

"You won't hear it from me," Mack said. "Brotherly loyalty and all that." His expression sobered. "But, Melanie, try to remember something—Richard is one of the good guys."

"I know that."

"Don't lose sight of it, no matter what happens, no matter how crazy things get around here, no matter what shenanigans Destiny is up to," he said urgently. "Richard presents this secure facade to the world, but he needs someone in his life who can see past his rock-solid wall of defenses."

"I'm helping him with his campaign," Melanie pointed out. "I'm not here for any other reason, despite what he may have told you."

Mack grinned. "The charade thing. Yeah, I know about that. Funny thing about charades. If you really throw yourself into one, the line between truth and fantasy starts to blur."

"Not for me," Melanie said confidently.

"Lucky you." He regarded her seriously. "Or maybe not."

Before she could ask what he meant by that, he was gone, whistling that chipper tune again. Apparently Mack was going to prove to be as annoyingly enigmatic as the rest of the Carltons.

Sighing, she continued on to Richard's office, rapped on the door, then stuck her head inside. "Okay to come in? Your secretary's not in yet."

Richard gave her a sour look. "She's not in because I'm not usually bombarded by visitors at this hour."

Melanie refused to be daunted by his mood. "I ran into Mack in the hall. Did you two have words?"

"Mack and I never have words," Richard said. "He never sticks around long enough to have words. He breezes in, stirs things up and takes off."

So that was it. She'd suspected as much. "He seemed to be in a very good mood."

"Of course he was. This was one of his better hit-and-run missions."

"What did he want?"

Richard's gaze narrowed. "Did you come over here at this hour to discuss my brother?"

"No, I came to get started on your marketing plans. All the rest is what's known in the civilized world as conversation, idle chitchat, small talk, whatever."

"I don't have time for chitchat." He gestured at the papers on his desk. "I've got a major division that's underperforming. I need to figure out why."

He could be telling the truth or it could be an excuse. Melanie couldn't tell from his bland expression. "Then I'll get out of your hair," she said easily. "When can we talk? I want to establish a plan, a budget, that kind of thing. If you have a campaign manager, I need to meet with him. He—or she—can take a lot of this strategy stuff off your shoulders."

Richard closed his eyes and rubbed his temples.

"Headache?" Melanie asked sympathetically. "Little wonder, given everything you have on your plate. How about some tea? If you have a kitchen around here somewhere, I can make it before I head back to my office."

"You're not here to make me tea, dammit!"

She stared at him until he sighed.

"Sorry. I shouldn't have snapped."

"True enough," she said, determined not to make more out of his lousy mood than necessary to make her point that she wouldn't accept it. "Is that a yes or a no on the tea?"

He gestured to a door across the room. "There's a kitchen setup in the conference room. There should be some tea in there. If you don't mind making it, I'd love some."

"Lemon, sugar, anything?"

"Nothing."

She went into the conference room, which was paneled and elegantly furnished. A lavish arrangement of fresh flowers sat in the center of the rosewood conference table. Anyone walking into the room would know that this was a top-flight company, run by people with taste and refinement. She wondered if that was Destiny's doing or Richard's.

The kitchenette had a two-burner stainless-steel stove, a matching stainless-steel refrigerator, a cupboard filled with fine china and crystal and a drawer filled with sterling silver place settings, everything necessary for entertaining well-heeled board members.

Melanie filled a teakettle with water and put it on to boil, then searched for the tea. She found a wooden tea chest with a dozen different blends, chose a packet of Earl Grey and then put it and a porcelain cup onto a small tray. When the water was ready she filled a matching porcelain teapot, added it to the tray and returned to Richard's office.

Without saying a word, she poured water over the tea bag, then backed away. "I'll wait to hear from your secretary about scheduling that meeting."

As she started past Richard, he snagged her hand. "I really am sorry. My head's throbbing, I'm in a lousy mood, but that's no excuse for biting your head off."

She smiled at him. "As long as you see that, there might be hope for you yet."

"Even I'm not too old to learn a thing or two," he said. "As long as you're here, why don't you stay and we can talk over some of your ideas? I don't have a meeting scheduled until eight-thirty."

"What about that pile of paperwork?"

"It can wait. I'm not thinking clearly enough to deal with it anyway."

Melanie nodded and sat down. "Okay, then, here are the things we need to nail down. How much time do you want me to spend on your marketing plan? Do you want an initial strategy that can be turned over to staff, or do you want me to stay on to coordinate it? Originally we talked about some consulting on Carlton Industries marketing, as well. Is that priority or is the campaign? I don't need answers right this second, but you do need to think about all this. I don't want to run up a bill, unless we've agreed on every aspect."

"I appreciate that," Richard said, regarding her with a vaguely surprised expression.

"What?"

"I didn't expect you to be so..." He faltered.

"Organized?" she suggested mildly. "Could be that first impression I made. I really am good at what I do. Destiny wasn't wrong about that."

"I'm beginning to see that." He reached for a stack of folders on the corner of his desk and passed them to her. "These are résumés for prospective campaign managers. Look 'em over and give me some input." He scanned his day planner. "We'll meet again at three. I'll be able to give you fifteen minutes, so be on time and keep it short. I've set up an office for you down the hall. You can use it when you're here. If you need anything that isn't there, tell Winifred, my secretary. She'll see that you have it. We'll deal with all the other issues once the campaign manager has been hired. He should be in on that meeting."

"Agreed," she said at once. "I'll see you at three, then."

She was almost out the door, when he called her back. "Yes?" she said.

"Do you have plans for dinner tonight?"

"Richard—"

He cut her off before she could voice the protest. "This is business. I have to attend a fund-raiser at eight. Destiny's co-chair. There will be a lot of people there you should get to know." He grinned. "And it will make Destiny happy to see you with me."

"Then the charade's still on?" she asked, not entirely sure how she felt about that. The dancing of her pulse suggested she was happier than she should be.

"Of course," he said. "We agreed to keep it up until she backs off."

Melanie was struck by a worrisome thought. "Have you considered what might happen if she discovers this was all a game being played out for her benefit?"

"Believe me, letting her find out is not an option," Richard said grimly. "That's why we can't let down our guard for a second. She'll be expecting me to bring you tonight."

At this rate, Melanie concluded that she was going to go broke buying an appropriate wardrobe for black-tie events. "What time?" she asked, resigned.

"I'll pick you up at seven-thirty."

Melanie nodded. "If there are more formal events like this where I'm going to be expected to show up on your arm, I'll need more notice. I don't have a fairy godmother who can magically make me look presentable."

His lips twitched. "Fair enough," he said. "But don't say that around Destiny. I have a hunch she'd be thrilled to be cast in the fairy-godmother role. Dressing three boys did not allow her to utilize her creative flair for fashion. No matter how ingenious the designer, a tux is still basically a tux."

Melanie laughed. "Yes, I imagine that could prove frustrating to a woman like Destiny." She tapped the folders in her arms. "I'd better get busy with these."

Richard nodded. "See you at three, then."

"Right."

Melanie backed out of his office and closed the door behind her, then leaned against it. There had been at least three occasions in there when she'd wanted to dive across that massive desk of his and kiss him till his expression brightened. That would have been about as smart as nose-diving off the top of the Washington Monument.

Now she was expected to spend yet another evening with Richard, pretending to be something more than a freelance marketing consultant, and at the end of the evening she was expected to go home—alone—and keep the man out of her dreams. If this kept up, she was going to have to talk to him about hazardous-duty pay. She could not see one single way that this was going to have anything other than a very unhappy ending.

Melanie sifted through the pile of résumés, making notes on those she felt to be the strongest candidates for running Richard's campaign. She also jotted on sticky notes and put them on each folder for those she considered wrong for the job. She wasn't sure how much Richard intended to rely on her opinion or whether this was some sort of test he'd devised to see if they were on the same wavelength, but she intended to give him a thoughtful, intelligent response on each applicant.

One or two were so inexperienced they were laughable, but most fell into the middle range, with adequate experience, bright ideas and ambition. There were three whose applications stood out. She put those folders on top, then rubbed her knotted shoulders. She'd been sitting too long. She'd skipped lunch, because she was so determined to do this assignment thoroughly and intelligently. She wanted badly to prove to Richard that he hadn't made a mistake in hiring her as a consultant, even if his motives for doing so had nothing at all to do with her qualifications for the job.

Becky poked her head into Melanie's office. "Safe to come in?" she asked.

"Sure."

Becky came in and sat down. "Tell me again why you're going through all those résumés."

"Richard asked for my input."

"So you immediately dropped everything to handle that?"

"I didn't drop everything," Melanie said defensively. "I rescheduled a couple of appointments. No big deal. It happens all the time."

"Something tells me it's going to be happening a lot more often now," Becky said.

"If it does, it's only because Richard will be paying us big bucks."

"To dance to his tune," Becky said. "I don't like it. Neither will all the people who've been paying us regularly for months or even years. They may be little fish, but they're *our* little fish."

"I'm not going to neglect them," Melanie vowed, then studied Becky's skeptical expression. "What's really going on, Becky? I thought you understood how important it was for us to nab this account."

"I don't like to see you jumping through hoops for this man. You're too good for that."

"It's not for some man," Melanie said. "It's for a client."

"Then the whole charade for his aunt's benefit is off?"

"Not exactly," she admitted.

"Figured as much," Becky said grimly. "And you don't see how risky that is? You're not the least bit attracted to him? This isn't at all personal?"

Melanie bit back the quick and easy lie that had formed. "Okay, maybe it is a little bit personal," she admitted. "A part of me does want to impress the daylights out of him. But it's not going to get out of hand."

Becky rolled her eyes. "It's been one day, sweetie, and in my humble opinion, it is already veering wildly out of control."

"Wildly?" Melanie scoffed. "I canceled a couple

of appointments and spent a few hours reading these files. Come on, Becky, that's not unreasonable when we take on a new client.''

''If you say so.''

''I do.'' Before she could say more, her private line rang. Melanie picked it up. ''Hello.''

''Ms. Hart?'' an unfamiliar female voice asked.

''Yes.''

''This is Winifred, Mr. Carlton's secretary. He asked me to tell you that he has to cancel the three-o'clock meeting, but he'll still pick you up at seven-thirty this evening.''

''I see,'' Melanie said, avoiding Becky's gaze. ''Thanks for calling.''

When she hung up, Becky gave her a knowing look. ''Meeting's off?''

Melanie nodded, feeling exactly like the idiot Becky so clearly thought she was.

''I notice you didn't jot down another time. Did he reschedule?''

''No. Maybe he intends to go over it tonight.''

''Tonight?''

Melanie winced at Becky's incredulous tone. ''I guess I forgot to mention the fund-raiser we're going to.''

Her friend merely shook her head. ''Yes, I'm sure he'll want you to share all your notes with him, while he's shaking hands with all the movers and shakers who'll be there.''

''We'll have time on the drive over,'' Melanie said with waning confidence. ''Or after.''

Becky gave her a pointed look. ''Mel, how far are you prepared to go to keep this stupid account?''

Melanie was stunned by her friend's implication. "What are you suggesting?"

"I'm suggesting that you're about to walk a very fine line here and, frankly, given that sparkle you get in your eye whenever Richard's name is mentioned, I'm not sure you won't tumble headfirst across it."

"That's an awful thing to say," Melanie said, genuinely hurt that Becky's opinion of her was so low.

"It's an awful thing to think," Becky said. "You're my dearest friend and I love you to pieces, but I'm absolutely terrified that you're about to do something you'll regret."

"Are you worried for me or for the business?" Melanie asked cynically.

"You, of course," Becky said without hesitation. "Though I have to think that your professional reputation could suffer, too, if people perceive that you're literally in bed with one of your major accounts."

"I am not sleeping with Richard," Melanie retorted.

"Yet," Becky said, not backing down.

"I've made it clear that I won't sleep with him," she insisted.

Becky sighed. "We're in a funny business, Mel. We spend a whole lot of time helping people to create a public perception. We're best at it when perception and reality are the same. We're both too honest to do a very good job of spinning the truth."

"In other words, if people suspect I'm sleeping with Richard, it won't matter if I'm not," Melanie said, defeated by what was obvious even to her.

"Bingo."

"How the hell did I get myself mixed up in this

mess?'' she asked a little plaintively, even though she knew the answer all too well. She'd caved to Destiny's sneakiness and Richard's insistence.

''That one's easy,'' Becky told her. ''You wanted to do a favor for a friend.'' She grinned. ''How were you supposed to know you'd fall head over heels in lust at first sight?''

''I'm not in love with Richard,'' Melanie said emphatically.

Becky's grin spread. ''I said *l-u-s-t,*'' she corrected. ''But I find it very interesting that that's not what you heard.'' She stood up. ''My work here is done. I'm going home.''

''It's not even three o'clock.''

''I know, but you need time to yourself to get all gussied up for tonight.''

''Maybe I should wear sackcloth,'' Melanie said.

''I doubt it would help. Something tells me Richard's too smitten to notice.''

''It's a charade, dammit!'' Melanie shouted, but Becky was already gone. Melanie heard her chuckling as Becky closed the front door behind her.

She scowled at the pile of résumés she'd wasted most of the day studying. It would serve Richard right if she told him to hire some inexperienced, incompetent idiot, but she wouldn't. She'd make him take her seriously yet. After all, Becky was right about one thing—when their farce of a relationship ended, she needed to make sure that her professional reputation emerged unscathed.

Chapter Ten

Richard knew he'd made a tactical mistake canceling that meeting with Melanie the instant he saw her face. There was no welcome in her expression, no hint of a sparkle in her eyes. She was cool, polite and about as distant as any stranger he'd ever met. If he didn't fix this fast, it was going to be a long evening.

Fortunately, he'd anticipated something like this and made a couple of quick adjustments to the evening's schedule. One wouldn't come into play until later, but for now he pulled an extravagant bouquet from behind his back. "I thought you might like these," he said, watching her closely for some sign that the gesture was making inroads.

"They're beautiful," she said softly, burying her face in the fragrant assortment of lilies and roses. "Let me put them in water." She fled the room without a backward glance.

Satisfied that at least she hadn't tossed the flowers right back in his face, Richard took the time to look around her living room, which he'd barely glimpsed on his earlier visit. He supposed it was done in that style they called shabby chic, an assortment of old and new pieces assembled with a certain flair for color. It was not something he would ever have chosen for his own decor, but it was surprisingly inviting. If this evening hadn't been so important to Destiny, he'd have been content to stay right here, even with Melanie's gaze shooting daggers at him.

He glanced around when she came back with the flowers in a large crystal vase. She set it in the middle of the low, glass-topped coffee table, then regarded him with another cool glance.

"We should be going," she said stiffly.

The formality grated. Richard couldn't seem to stop himself from reaching for her. "Not until I've gotten this out of the way," he murmured right before he kissed her.

She resisted for half a heartbeat, then sighed against his lips. When he finally released her, she stared at him with more heat in her eyes.

"You don't play fair," she accused.

"Only as a last resort," he said. "I couldn't think of another way to cut through all that ice."

"You could have said you were sorry about canceling that meeting after I spent the entire day preparing for it," she said. "It made me wonder if you really cared about my input after all. This deal of ours is only going to work if you take me seriously. Otherwise, I want out now."

He'd guessed that would be her interpretation. "Of course I do, or I wouldn't have asked for it," he reassured her. "If we're going to work together, you need to understand that my schedule changes all the time. It's a fact of life. I have to respond to emergencies, react to last-second opportunities. I had two hours to get an offer on the table for a company I've been after for years. We really had to scramble once we found out there was a chance the management might look favorably on an offer from us in order to stave off a hostile bid from someone else. I was in with the attorneys right up until the deadline at five o'clock."

Melanie looked somewhat satisfied with the explanation. "Okay, I overreacted, probably because I saw this as my first big chance to impress you. Plus, you seemed to take it for granted that I'd drop everything to get ready for that meeting, and you didn't even bother to have your secretary reschedule."

"Because I was going to see you tonight myself. I was hoping the flowers would get me off the hook," he said.

"Admittedly, they were a nice touch," she told him, a smile finally teasing at her lips. "But a few sincere words would have been better." She gazed into his eyes. "Then, again, I imagine you're not used to apologizing to anyone for your actions, are you?"

"I do when it's necessary," he said, disconcerted by her too-accurate assessment. He wasn't used to anyone questioning his actions. What was it Destiny had said, that too many people bowed to his every whim? Taking another person's feelings into consideration was going to be a new—and most likely humbling—experience, at least if tonight was any example.

"Which you deem to be the case how often?" Melanie inquired tartly. "Once a year? Less?"

"Less," he admitted with a shrug. "I am sorry for canceling the meeting. My schedule was too tight in the first place, even without that unexpected opportunity to bid on the company I want. I should never have scheduled another meeting, but I knew how anxious you were to get started and I wanted you to see that I intend to listen to your advice."

For the first time since his arrival, her expression brightened. "You do?"

Richard laughed. "Don't let it go to your head. I said I'd listen, not that I'd act on it."

She grinned. "That's a start. I thought you were just dismissing me today because you figured whatever I had to say wasn't important."

"Honestly, Melanie, I do want to hear your impressions. You can tell me in the car."

"How far away is this fund-raiser?"

"Ten minutes."

She nodded. "I'll talk fast. There are only a few people worth talking about anyway."

When they walked outside, she stopped and stared at the limo waiting by the curb. "Very fancy."

"I find it useful when I hope to get some work done." He met her gaze as he ushered her into the luxurious car. "Or when I want to devote all of my attention to the person I'm with."

"Oh, boy," she murmured. "How am I supposed to concentrate after you say something sweet like that?"

"We could just put aside all these pesky business things till later and go back to kissing," he suggested slyly. He was fairly certain he'd never get enough of kissing her.

When he started to lean toward her, she held him back. "I don't think so. You didn't hire me for my kissing prowess."

He laughed. "You sure about that? We do have two deals, you know."

She gave him a look filled with confusion. "Believe me, that has not slipped my mind for a single second. Something tells me it's going to be keeping me awake at night."

Richard bit back another laugh. "Trust me, sweetheart, I've had the same thought." He regarded her hopefully. "If we're going to be awake anyway, we could spend the night doing something interesting."

She gave him a look clearly meant to freeze his libido in its tracks.

"I don't think so," she said icily.

Richard might have taken her at her word if there hadn't been the tiniest flicker of pure fire in her eyes. He was counting on that flame to defrost all that ice eventually. He just prayed he could manage to control himself till then. Exercising his restraint was getting to be more difficult with every second he spent with her.

Melanie was startled when the first person they ran into as they entered the hotel ballroom was Mack. He seemed to be on the lookout for them, because he instantly latched on to Richard's arm and pulled them right back into the bustling corridor, where a half-dozen registration tables had been set up so people could pick up their table assignments.

"Brace yourselves," he said grimly. "Pete Forsythe is here, looking like a cat who was let free in the aviary. One glimpse of you two and he'll have the lead for tomorrow morning's column.''

"Won't that be fun?'' Melanie muttered, then brightened. "We could use this, you know.''

Richard and Mack both stared at her.

"How?'' Richard asked.

"He wants a juicy tidbit. Let's give him one. Let's end the speculation right here and now and tell him that you are definitely considering a run for Alexandria City Council and that you've hired me to advise you.''

Richard was already shaking his head. "I'm not ready to announce that yet, not without a campaign manager in place, and we're at least a couple of weeks away from that. The earliest I intend to announce is mid-January.''

"You're not announcing it,'' Melanie explained patiently. "You're only conceding what everyone already knows, that you're *thinking* about running. Then you acknowledge our business relationship and, *poof,* we get rid of the speculation about a romance. The truth will be so boring, he might not even print it.''

Mack laughed. "Very clever. Listen to her, Richard. I know this guy. He thrives on scandal and innuendo. This will sound way too tame for his readers.''

Richard finally nodded. "Okay, then, let's go feed him this dull little tidbit and pray that Destiny hasn't seen fit to give him an entirely different scoop.''

"Such as?'' Melanie asked, not entirely sure she wanted to know the answer.

"News of our imminent engagement," Richard said.

"She's seen us together once," Melanie pointed out.

"But she has an active imagination," Mack said. "And she does love to embroider the truth when it suits her purposes. If she has a chance to prod along this budding romance, she'll grab it. Unfortunately, Richard has a point, too."

"We could duck out right now, before Forsythe sees us," Richard suggested.

"No way," Melanie said, refusing to be daunted by Richard and Mack's dire predictions. "That's exactly the wrong thing to do. If Forsythe hears we were here or has caught even a glimpse of us, he'll go wild wondering why we disappeared during the hors d'oeuvres. He'll probably run right into the lobby to check the guest register to see if we slipped away upstairs."

"Our names won't be there," Richard reminded her, then grinned. "Unless…"

"Forget that," she said succinctly as Mack tried to smother a laugh. "Besides, it won't matter what he finds. He'll just conclude you bribed the desk clerk. Tomorrow morning we'll be reading all about how we disappeared to be alone together. I still think my original plan is best. We have to march in there as if we have absolutely nothing to hide, which we don't. Beyond that, it's a very crowded room. It's possible we can meet and greet, make our presence felt and get out without ever crossing paths with Forsythe. He can pick up the word about why we're here together from other sources."

Mack nodded his agreement. "I'm with Melanie,

bro. I'll go in first and run interference," he suggested with a look of pure anticipation.

Richard frowned at him. "I thought you always hid behind those huge offensive linesmen."

"Very funny," Mack retorted. "Either way, I'm more experienced at this sort of thing than you are."

"Running interference or avoiding Pete Forsythe's speculation?" Richard asked.

"Both," Mack said succinctly.

"By the way, where's your date?" Richard asked.

"I came alone," Mack said. "Less fodder for Destiny. Besides, I didn't want to steal your limelight." He grinned. "You know, in case you decided tonight was the night to make your big announcement."

Richard gave him a dire look. "You are going to be such dead meat when Destiny sets her sights on your love life. I'm going to help her in every way I can."

Melanie grinned at the brotherly byplay. "Richard, I'm not so sure it's wise to antagonize the man who's going to throw himself between us and Pete Forsythe."

Richard held up his hands. "Okay, okay. Do your thing, little brother. Get us to Destiny unscathed."

Mack proved to be remarkably adept at maneuvering through the crowd. Apparently all that experience eluding tackles was paying off, Melanie concluded as they made their way toward the head table where Destiny was holding court with several distinguished-looking gentlemen. To Melanie's astonishment, she realized that two of them were senators and one was a top aide to the president. She suddenly felt as if she'd fallen down the rabbit hole and landed at the

Mad Hatter's tea party. She was definitely out of her usual element in such lofty company.

Destiny welcomed them with a beaming smile, then performed the introductions with a graciousness that made Melanie sound as if she owned a top-flight firm on New York's Madison Avenue. The men regarded her with an automatic respect she wasn't used to garnering after an introduction. She was used to having to prove herself and her right to work in such exalted circles. Heck, she still hadn't proved herself to Richard.

"Richard, you fox," Senator Furhman said. "Leave it to you to find someone who's beautiful, smart and talented, while the rest of us are stuck getting advice from balding old fogies."

Melanie waited to hear what Richard would say to that. It would tell her a lot about his diplomacy and tact, to say nothing of hinting at his opinion of her professional skills. Not that he had much to go on yet.

He met the senator's gaze. "I'd recommend you hire her yourself," he said, then grinned. "But not until I'm in office."

"Then you are definitely running for Council in Alexandria?" the presidential aide asked.

"Definitely considering it," Richard admitted as he and Melanie had just agreed.

Listening to him, she decided he was going to be a quick study, which would make her job much easier.

"Why not for Congress?" Senator Furhman asked. "Waste of time, a man of your caliber starting at the bottom like that."

"Public service at any level is never a waste of time," Richard said, an edge in his voice.

"Well, of course not," all three men were quick to say.

Melanie grinned at the smooth way Richard had put them in their place without overtly offending them or suggesting that their own ambitions were in any way suspect. He was going to be a good candidate, no question about it. No one would rattle him.

"Gentlemen, if you'll excuse us, Melanie and I have things to discuss tonight." He leaned down and gave his aunt a kiss. "Sorry. We can't stay."

Melanie and Mack both gave him a startled look. Richard merely gave them an enigmatic smile.

"You ready, sweetheart?" he asked her.

The seemingly deliberate use of the endearment caught Melanie off guard. It was impossible to tell if it had been meant for Destiny's benefit or for that of her friends or maybe even for Pete Forsythe's ears.

"Darling," Richard prodded when she remained silent. "Ready?"

Melanie nodded numbly. "Sure."

Not until they were outside in the cold night air waiting for the limo to reappear did she face him and demand, "What was that about?"

"You mean the hasty exit?"

"That and the hint that we had more fascinating ways to spend the evening? I thought we'd decided that was a bad message to be putting out there."

"You thought so. I don't. Besides, this message was specifically for my aunt. We've agreed to that," he said.

Melanie wasn't appeased. "You said it in front of

witnesses, who are even now probably seeking out Forsythe to spill what they heard.''

''I'm tired of worrying about him.''

''You have to worry about him,'' Melanie said impatiently. ''You have to use the media to get *your* message across, not feed their appetite for intrigue. I thought you'd promised to listen to my advice.''

''I did, which is why we got out of there, so I can listen to what you have to say and hear myself think.'' He opened the door of the limo for her. ''I'm starved. Why don't we pick up something and take it back to your place?''

Melanie frowned at the suggestion. ''You're not getting any crazy ideas of a personal nature, are you?''

He laughed. ''Several of them, to be honest, but I'll settle for going over those résumés.''

She shook her head. ''You really know how to show a girl a good time.''

''Before you get too huffy, wait till you see what I have in mind for takeout,'' he said. ''I guarantee you'll like it better than the rubber chicken on the menu back there.''

''If you say so,'' she said, still not entirely convinced that he wasn't up to no good.

He settled Melanie in the limo, then went up front to have a private word with the driver. When he came back, he said, ''He'll drop us off, then bring back dinner.''

Melanie knew she ought to be ecstatic that they were no longer under Destiny's watchful eye and were far from Pete Forsythe's speculative gaze. She ought to be even happier that they were actually going to talk business.

Instead, all she could think about was how dangerous it was going to be for her to be alone with Richard with no one around to stop her if either one of them lost control of their apparently madcap hormones.

"You're going to want to change out of that dress before dinner," Richard said the minute they walked into Melanie's living room.

She gave him a suspicious look. "Oh?"

He grinned. "I'm not telling you to slip into something more comfortable," he chided. "Though if that's what you want to do, I won't object. I have a particular fondness for women in satin and lace."

"Don't get your hopes up," she retorted. "I'm thinking a sweat suit."

To her surprise, he grinned. "Make it an old one."

"Why?"

"That dinner I ordered doesn't exactly mix with high fashion. Of course, if you want to live dangerously…" His voice trailed off.

Melanie stared at him. She couldn't quite get a fix on this oddly playful mood of his. "What on earth did you order?" she asked suspiciously.

"It's a surprise. I think you'll be very happy."

"You don't know enough about my taste in food to be able to make that claim," she retorted.

"Sure, I do."

"How?"

"You have your resources. I have mine. Unless you intend to be totally stubborn, go change. I'll fix us a drink. Do you have any red wine?"

She actually had several bottles of the wine she knew he preferred. She was not proud of the fact that she'd gone out and bought them, hoping for an occasion like this.

"There's a wine rack in the kitchen," she told him. "The selection's hardly as extensive as what you must have, but there's bound to be something there that will do."

Relieved to have him occupied, she fled to her room to change. She abandoned the baggy sweat suit idea—she did have some pride, after all—and settled for a comfortable pair of slim-fitting jeans and a becoming russet sweater.

She was on her way back to the living room, when the doorbell rang. The chauffeur stood on the stoop with two huge insulated bags designed to keep carryout food hot. Melanie stared at the familiar logo on the bags, mouth gaping.

"You ordered barbecue?" she asked as Richard came up behind her and took the bags. "From Ohio?"

"Your assistant said you go into raptures every time you talk about it," he said. "I figured I owed you something after canceling that meeting. I wanted to make you smile." He studied her intently. "You're not smiling yet."

"Give me a minute," she said, still wrestling with the appearance of food from an Ohio restaurant on her doorstep as if it were being delivered around the corner. "When on earth did you talk to Becky?"

"About twenty minutes before I had my secretary call and cancel the meeting. Once I spoke with Becky, I wanted to be sure I could pull this off before I had Winifred call you. I knew you'd be disappointed in me, and I wanted to make up for that."

"Oh, my God," she whispered. No wonder Becky

had been so worried earlier. She'd already spoken to Richard and knew he was planning this extravagant surprise. Becky also knew how Melanie was likely to react to a man who did something this totally unexpected and extraordinary.

Richard studied her with a narrowed gaze. "You're still not smiling. You do like this barbecue, right?"

"It's amazing," she said. "It's one of the things I miss most about home."

"That's what Becky said."

"But for you to go to all this trouble," she said, still stunned. "It must have cost a fortune to have this flown in."

"That's what corporate jets are for. Next time, we'll fly over and eat there. You can see your family."

Feeling totally dazed, Melanie turned around and walked past him. Until this instant she hadn't comprehended what it meant to be a man like Richard Carlton, a man who could do something this outrageous on a whim. She'd been frightened by her growing feelings for him before. Now she was terrified. It would be way too easy to be seduced by grand gestures like this and forget all about the dangers of getting seriously involved with the man making them.

She sat down at the kitchen table, picked up her glass of wine and took a careful sip to steady her nerves. Richard put the bags on the table, sat down opposite her and regarded her worriedly.

"Are you upset about this? I thought I was doing something nice."

Melanie met his gaze and finally allowed herself a small smile. "You did. In fact, no one has ever done anything so incredibly sweet and nice and over-the-top for me before.''

"Okay, I'll confess I'm new to this. Is that a bad thing?" he asked.

"It could be," she admitted, her smile fading.

"Why?"

"It's wildly seductive," she said before she could censor herself.

"Oh, really?" he said, clearly intrigued. "How seductive?"

She gave him a scolding look. "Don't even go there. I meant that I don't know what to do with it."

He regarded her blankly. "Eat it. In fact, if the aroma coming out of these bags is anything to go by, that is definitely what we should do with it."

"I meant I don't know how to handle a gesture like this," she said impatiently. "It's too much."

"It's dinner."

"From *Ohio!* From my favorite restaurant, where I used to go with all my friends when we wanted to celebrate a special occasion."

"Would you have been happier if I'd brought in Chinese from down the block?"

"Not happier," she admitted. "But that would have made sense."

He reached for her hand, then pressed a kiss against her knuckles. "That would have been safe, that's what you really mean, isn't it? It would have been ordinary, acceptable, not scary."

She nodded slowly, trying not to notice that he was still holding her hand, that he was still sending shivers down her spine just with that touch.

"Why are you so desperate to feel safe around me?"

"Because we're playing a game, Richard," she said a little desperately. "That's what we agreed to."

"And barbecue from Ohio changes the rules?"

"Pretty much," she said, afraid she was sounding both ungrateful and ridiculous.

"Want me to throw it out?" he asked, picking up the bags.

Reacting purely to the needy growling in her stomach that came with each whiff of the familiar food, she grabbed the bags away from him. "Don't you dare. I don't pretend to know why you really did this, but I want that barbecue."

He grinned. "Shall I get the napkins?"

"Get lots of them, because this is not food that can be eaten neatly," she said, opening the bags to find enough baby-back ribs, coleslaw, potato salad and corn bread to feed a half-dozen people. She looked at Richard incredulously. "Were you expecting company?"

"I figured if it was that good, you'd want leftovers." He grinned. "Besides, Becky made me promise there would be some for her in return for her not telling you what I was up to."

Melanie shook her head. "If she can bamboozle you to make a deal like that, maybe I should send her out to negotiate our contracts from now on."

"I think you do okay on your own," he told her.

"Thank you." She looked him over. "If you expect to have a prayer of staying clean, lose the tie, roll up your sleeves and tuck a napkin in your collar."

He grinned and did as she'd instructed. He immediately looked more casual, more relaxed…more seductive. Lord, give me strength, she prayed. "And thank you for this food," she added aloud.

Richard gave her a questioning look.

"Just saying a little blessing before dinner," she said.

Judging from the amusement flickering in his eyes, she had a hunch he knew that was only a small part of what she'd been praying for.

"Melanie?"

"Hmm?" she murmured distractedly as she took her first bite of the tender, perfectly seasoned pork. She had to stop herself from moaning with pleasure.

"Look at me," Richard commanded.

She met his gaze and nearly shuddered at the heat she saw there. "What?"

"Fair warning. I usually do safe and I usually do ordinary, but you seem to inspire me to go beyond that."

She swallowed hard and nodded. "Yes, I think I get that now." Heaven help her.

Chapter Eleven

Richard was not the least bit surprised to find Destiny waiting for him when he arrived at his office the next morning. He'd known that her curiosity would get the better of her. It was not every night that he slipped out of a major social event attended by business and political leaders to be with a woman. He'd calculated the effect before he'd done it. That one move alone was going to convince his aunt he was serious about Melanie.

Unfortunately, the fact that it had started as a game to get Destiny to back off was beginning to get a little fuzzy in his head. At some point last night, things had turned serious, at least for him. Until he understood why that was, he was going to be doing a delicate balancing act between convincing Destiny the romance was real and assuring Melanie that it was not. Damn, but subterfuge was complicated. That's why he'd spent his life avoiding it, in business and in his personal life.

"Did you and Melanie enjoy your evening?" Destiny asked without preamble. The glint of anticipation in her eyes suggested she was hoping for some very juicy details.

"Very much," he said neutrally.

"Did you do anything special?"

Richard gave her a sharp look. "You know about dinner, don't you?"

His aunt grinned. "That you flew it in from her favorite teen hangout in Ohio? Yes, I did hear about that. I must commend you, Richard. It was a nice touch, something I might have dreamed up had you asked for my input."

"Is everybody in my company on your payroll, too?"

"If you're asking if they all spy for me, the answer is no. I just make it my business to stay well-informed where my nephews are concerned. It's amazing how cooperative some people are willing to be when you're pleasant to them."

He heard the implied criticism, but he was in no mood for it. "You need to get your own life and stay out of mine."

She shrugged. "Maybe one of these days, when I'm satisfied that you, Mack and Ben are happy."

"We'd be a lot happier without you poking around in our personal lives."

"Really?" she asked doubtfully. "You'd never have met Melanie if not for me. Can you honestly say you were happier before she came along?"

"I was at peace," he said, trying to recall what that had felt like. Probably lonely, if he were to be totally honest about it. Melanie hadn't been around all that long, but he was already having difficulty imagining his life without her.

"Darling, that's not the same thing at all," Destiny said. "In fact, it seems to me you had a little too much peace in your life."

"I was content with that," he said, even though he knew he was not only lying but wasting his breath.

"Well, Melanie's in your life now," Destiny said breezily. "I hope you won't do anything foolish to ruin it."

"I doubt you'll give me a chance," he muttered.

She chuckled. "Not if I can help it. Christmas is coming, you know. Will Melanie be joining us next week?"

"You mean for the traditional Carlton excess?"

She frowned at the edge in his voice. "I love the holidays. Sue me. And despite your sour mood this morning, you usually do, as well."

She was right, though Richard had no intention of giving her the satisfaction of admitting it. "I assume if I don't invite Melanie myself, you'll do it behind my back," he grumbled, even though he'd already planned to include Melanie in their Christmas Eve and Christmas Day celebrations. Let Destiny believe he was making a huge concession just for her benefit.

"I'm hoping that it won't be necessary for me to go behind your back," she said mildly. "Remember dinner's at eight on Christmas Eve. Then I expect you all back for brunch at eleven on Christmas Day. We'll open our gifts then. Be sure to get something special for Melanie. Do it yourself. Don't leave it to Winifred."

"I think I can remember the schedule," he said,

ignoring the barb about assigning his shopping to his secretary. "We've been doing the same thing for twenty years."

"Tradition is important. Someday you'll appreciate that."

Richard supposed that was possible. He'd never given it much thought before. For a moment his imagination took flight and he pictured years of family traditions created with Melanie for their family. As soon as the thought crept in, he stamped it out. He was getting carried away. If he wasn't careful, this whole charade thing was going to get out of hand. Maybe that's what Melanie had been trying to tell him last night, that it was *already* out of hand. If so, he was very much afraid she'd gotten it exactly right.

"Richard's on line one," Becky announced with surprisingly good cheer when Melanie walked into her house after a meeting with a client she'd been putting off ever since Richard's business had taken over most of the minutes of her day.

Becky held out the phone. "You want to take it here?" she asked, her expression hopeful.

Melanie shook her head. "I'll get it in a sec," she said, wanting to figuratively catch her breath before speaking to the man who'd literally taken it away the night before with his wildly impulsive gesture.

"Once you two have talked, you can tell me all about dinner last night," Becky added. "I can't wait to hear every little detail. I've asked, but Richard doesn't seem inclined to spill the beans on whether he got lucky."

"Good God, please tell me you didn't ask him that," Melanie said.

"Not in those exact words," Becky said, grinning.

At last, some evidence of discretion and good sense, Melanie thought. Avoiding Becky's probing questions was also a rather powerful incentive for keeping Richard on hold indefinitely. She did not want to engage in a postmortem with a woman who knew her as well as Becky did. Becky would see straight through any attempts to deny that she was falling for Richard.

"I think I'll take the call in my office," Melanie said, walking into the room and firmly closing the door behind her.

She heard Becky's indignant gasp as the door clicked shut.

When Melanie felt reasonably composed, she picked up the receiver. "Good morning," she said briskly, determined to keep things cool and professional this morning, the exact opposite of the way they'd been the night before. "Sorry to keep you waiting. I'm just back from a meeting."

"No problem. How are you?"

"Doing great. You?"

"Fine," he said, sounding amused. "Is Becky standing over your shoulder listening to every word? She seems awfully curious about last night."

"I think that's to be expected under the circumstances, since you saw fit to take her into your confidence."

"You have a point," he conceded. "I won't make that mistake again. You didn't say, though. Is she there?"

"No, as a matter of fact, I shut the door to my office. I don't think she can hear me, though I imagine her ear's pressed against the door," she said a bit more loudly.

The comment was greeted by an indignant huff from the outer office.

"Now, then what can I do for you?" she asked Richard.

"We need to talk about Christmas," he said. "It's next week."

Melanie bit back a smile. "So I've heard. I'm surprised you remember. Winifred must have made a note on your calendar."

"Actually Destiny was here this morning," he said.

"So that explains your sudden recollection of the holiday," she teased. "Family prompting. Did she ask you to pass it on to all the other workaholics you know?"

"No, but she is expecting you to join us for Christmas Eve dinner and brunch on Christmas Day," he said. "I promised to invite you."

Melanie was completely caught off guard. Spend the holiday with his family? She wasn't sure she could pull that off. It seemed way too…intimate. "Isn't that carrying things a bit too far?"

"Not if we expect to convince Destiny we have a real relationship. You're not going home to visit your family, are you?"

"No, but—"

"Then there's no reason you can't join us. I'll give my aunt credit for one thing—she does do the holidays up right. You'll have a good time and, goodness knows, you'll get plenty to eat."

"It's not being entertained or fed that I'm worried about."

"Then what is it?"

"It's a lie, Richard. On Christmas," she added, as if that were somehow worse than all the other lying going on.

"I see your point."

"Do you really?"

"Believe it or not, I'm not in the habit of lying to people myself," he said. "These are extraordinary times."

"Not that extraordinary," she insisted. "How can we keep this up? I'm getting more uncomfortable all the time."

She waited through a long silence.

"Maybe we need to speed up the timetable a bit," he suggested finally.

Melanie wasn't reassured by his cautious tone. "Meaning?"

"Let me give this some more thought," he said. "Just promise you'll be there."

"I don't suppose these will be huge gatherings where I can get lost in the crowd," she asked, hopeful.

"Afraid not. The bashes come between Christmas and New Year's. These two occasions are just for family."

"Oh, God," Melanie murmured. "Richard, are you really sure about this?"

"I don't see an alternative," he told her, not sounding nearly as dismayed as he should have. "It would be highly unusual if you weren't there. In fact, it would be tantamount to an admission that we're not serious."

"You aren't beginning to enjoy this predicament we're in, are you?" she asked suspiciously.

"It's a necessary evil," he claimed, though he didn't sound very sincere. "Trust me."

"Trust you?" she echoed doubtfully.

"I haven't been wrong about Destiny so far, have I? She's behaving totally predictably."

"I suppose."

"Relax, Melanie, this won't be so bad. You know Destiny and Mack. The only person you haven't met is Ben, and he'll probably study you appreciatively with his artist's eye and never say two words."

"Are you telling me there's a member of the Carlton clan who isn't glib?"

Richard fell silent for so long, Melanie was afraid she'd said something dreadfully wrong. "Richard?"

"Ben used to be as chatty as the rest of us," he said slowly. "He's had a tough time the last couple of years."

"What happened?"

"He doesn't discuss it, so we don't, either. I'm sorry I can't prepare you any better than that. If it'll ease your mind any, you should know that he's the handsomest one of us all."

"Quiet, rich and gorgeous. I could be in love," Melanie joked.

"Don't get any ideas," Richard said. "You're wildly in love with me, remember?"

"Oh, right," she said. "Sometimes I lose track of the details in our arrangement."

"Very amusing," he said without the faintest hint of humor in his voice. "I guess Christmas would be a good time to put a spin on this you won't be able to forget."

Something in his tone alerted her that he was dead serious. "Richard, what is that supposed to mean?"

"Christmas is coming," he said. "It's not the time to ask a lot of questions."

Her heart took a sudden stutter-step. "Richard, don't you dare do anything foolish."

"Of course not. I'm stodgy, remember?"

He hung up abruptly before she could remind him that there had been nothing stodgy about his grand gesture the night before, nor about any of the kisses they'd shared. She had a sudden sinking sensation that he was about to top himself. The thought scared her to death.

Melanie was wearing a simply cut emerald velvet suit she'd found at Chez Deux when Richard picked her up on Christmas Eve. She looked amazing. She also looked a little as if she were being carted off to the guillotine. He regretted that he was the cause of that.

"There's no reason to look so terrified," he reassured her. "It's just dinner."

She gave him a skeptical look. "How many courses?"

"I have no idea. I never counted. What does that have to do with anything?"

"Just dinner is meat, potatoes, vegetables and maybe a pumpkin pie for dessert. Is that what we're likely to have tonight?"

He grinned. "Doubtful. Okay, I see your point." She'd been making quite a lot of good ones lately.

"Do you really? Something tells me that this meal is also going to be accompanied by a lot of expectant stares," she told him.

"Could be."

"And that doesn't scare you?"

"This is my family. They don't scare me," he insisted.

"Not even Destiny?"

He laughed. "Oh, well, if we're talking about Destiny specifically, she has put the fear of God into me from time to time."

"Especially lately, I imagine."

"Actually I've been warming to her mission," he said mildly, just as he pulled his car into the garage.

Melanie stared at him, obviously convinced she couldn't possibly have heard him correctly. He took some satisfaction in having caught her off guard.

"What did you just say?" she demanded.

He pretended not to hear her as he exited the car and went around to hold her door. She didn't budge.

"I asked you a question," she said, frowning up at him.

"We'll discuss it later," he promised. "We don't want to keep everyone waiting."

"Something tells me it would be smarter if we did," she grumbled, but she did get out of the car.

Inside, they found the rest of the family already gathered. Even Ben had put on a tux for the occasion, but he still wore his usual dour expression. Richard worried about the fact that Ben still hadn't snapped out of his dark, brooding mood, but Destiny insisted that people recovered from tragedy at their own pace.

At least Ben made an effort to smile when Destiny introduced him to Melanie.

"I've heard a lot about you," Ben said.

Melanie glanced at Richard, then back at Ben. "Really?"

"Actually, it's my aunt who's been singing your praises. Mack is entirely too absorbed with his own women to mention that Richard is involved with someone, and Richard only calls to see if I've remembered to come out of my studio long enough to eat.''

Melanie grinned. ''I've heard you're a talented artist. I'd love to see your work.''

To Richard's astonishment, Ben nodded.

''Come out to the farm sometime,'' he told her. ''I'm sure Destiny will bring you.''

''If anyone brings her, it'll be me,'' Richard grumbled, oddly disconcerted by the fact that Ben seemed to have taken an instant liking to Melanie. He studied his brother, trying to pinpoint whether his overall outlook had changed or whether this was purely a reaction to Melanie. He couldn't tell. He hadn't expected both of his brothers to be thoroughly besotted by her within minutes. Good thing he'd made his own plans to stake his claim.

''I thought you didn't let strangers poke around in your studio,'' Richard said.

Ben smiled with more animation than Richard had seen in months.

''But Melanie's not a stranger, is she? From what I gather she's practically family,'' he said in a tone that sounded almost like the Ben of old, full of life and mischief.

Destiny had filled him in, all right, Richard thought grimly. Or Mack. Either way, Ben seemed to be enjoying it, and that counted for a lot these days.

Melanie linked her arm through Ben's. ''Don't believe everything you hear,'' she confided. ''Some people are more confident than they should be. Now, would you mind pouring me a glass of wine, since your brother hasn't seen fit to do it yet?''

"It would be my pleasure," Ben said, crossing the room with her.

Richard stared after them in amazement. Even Mack looked astonished.

"Stop gaping," Destiny scolded. "Richard, you of all people should know what an amazing woman Melanie is."

"I had no idea she was a miracle worker," he mumbled, his gaze still following her as she chatted with his brother. Seeing her work her magic on Ben reassured him that his plan for tomorrow's family gathering was a wise one. It was time to raise the stakes. He simply wasn't sure anymore whether it had anything at all to do with Destiny.

Melanie felt like the worst sort of fraud. She was beginning to hate this stupid agreement she'd made with Richard to deceive Destiny into thinking they were getting serious about each other. Half a dozen times the night before, she'd been tempted to spill the truth and let the chips fall where they may, but she hadn't been able to bring herself to utter the words. She had a feeling her reticence was just the tiniest bit self-serving. She liked Richard. She liked his family. And some part of her that was doomed to heartbreak didn't want the charade to end.

She suspected that Richard knew that, too, and was using it to keep her in the game. He was sneaky like that, not in a mean way, but to protect his own interests. Whatever those interests were. She was no longer sure about that, not after some of the hints he'd been dropping lately. And not after he'd kissed her for so long the night before, church bells had been chiming the end of midnight services when he'd stopped. At least, she hoped those were the bells she'd heard ringing. Otherwise, she was in more trouble than she'd imagined.

"I should not be doing this," she told herself even as she showered and began dressing to return to Destiny's for Christmas brunch. "Nothing good can come from it." She stared at her reflection in the steamy bathroom mirror and nodded agreement, then sighed. "But I'm going anyway." Her tone was more resigned than defiant.

Once she was dressed, she made calls to her family to wish them a happy holiday.

"We miss you," her mother said. "When are you coming home?"

"Soon, I hope," Melanie promised, feeling instantly homesick.

"Stop pestering the girl," her father said. "She's busy. She'll come when she can."

"Thanks, Dad. I love you guys."

"What are you doing today?" her mother asked.

Now there was a quagmire if ever she'd seen one, Melanie thought. "Having brunch with friends," she said neutrally.

"Anyone we know?" her mother wanted to know.

"No."

"You're pestering again, Adele."

Her mother chuckled. "How am I supposed to find out anything, if I don't ask? Melanie never volunteers anything. She's exactly like you."

"Then that should tell you that poking and prodding won't get you what you want to know," her dad countered. "You ever have any luck with that with me?"

"Now that you mention it, no," her mother said. "Okay, I'll give up for now, since it's Christmas."

"Probably the best gift you've ever given the girl," Melanie's father teased.

"Oh, Dad, it is not," Melanie said, laughing at the familiar bickering. "Be nice, or she'll cut you off without any pumpkin pie."

"Never happen," he said. "She knows I've got her present hidden away where she'll never find it and she's not getting it till I've had my pie."

"You two are a riot," Melanie said. "How do you do it?"

"Do what?" her mother asked, sounding puzzled.

"Stay married for all these years and have so much fun with each other," Melanie elaborated.

"Why, we love each other, of course," her mother said.

"Indeed we do," her father agreed. "And she's never stopped laughing at my jokes. Laughter may be the most important thing there is in a relationship, aside from love."

"And trust," her mother said. "Don't forget that." She hesitated. "I don't suppose you're asking because there's somebody special in your life?"

Melanie sighed.

"There she goes again," her father said at once. "Say goodbye, Adele."

"It was worth a try," her mother grumbled. "Merry Christmas, darling!"

"Merry Christmas," Melanie said, slowly hanging up the phone, her eyes suddenly stinging with tears. Now she was deceiving her parents, too, at least by omission.

She was still swiping at the tears when she went to

answer the door. Richard took one look at her and pulled her into his arms without comment. She clung to him and let the tears flow.

When she finally stopped crying, she backed away, avoiding his gaze. "I'm sorry."

"Homesick?" he guessed.

That was only part of it, but she nodded, surprised by his understanding. "I just got off the phone with my folks."

He studied her face, then brushed away one last stray tear. "I could have you in Ohio in an hour."

She stared at him, astonished. "You would do that?"

"If it would put a smile back on your face."

Once more she was reminded of what it was like to know someone who could make such an offer so casually. "You will never know how much it means to me that you would do that, but I'm okay. I'll get home soon."

"You sure?"

"Yes," she said, feeling a hundred-percent better knowing that she could have gone home if it was what she'd truly wanted. It made the waiting easier. "Let me check my makeup and get my presents, then I'll be ready to go. I'm dying to see what you got your family for Christmas." She grinned. "I'll bet you're dying to see them open their gifts, too."

"I'll have you know that I went shopping," he called after her as she went into the bathroom.

Melanie laughed. "But did you actually buy anything?"

"Yes," he insisted. "You'll see. I promise you, you'll be impressed. I even did my own gift wrapping."

"I can hardly wait to see it," she said as she finished touching up the mess her tears had made of her makeup.

On her way back to the living room, she picked up her own token gifts for the Carltons and grabbed her coat.

"Did I mention that you look lovely?" Richard asked as he helped her on with her coat.

"No, but maybe that's because I was bawling my eyes out when you came in."

"You looked lovely even then," he assured her.

Feeling suddenly lighthearted, she patted his cheek. "Just for that, I hope Santa is very good to you."

His gaze caught hers and lingered until she felt heat rise in her cheeks.

"Something tells me it's going to be the best Christmas ever," he said quietly.

Melanie had that exact same feeling.

Brunch was yet another gourmet meal, evidently prepared by Destiny herself. She'd given the cook the holiday off.

"Why should she be working on Christmas, when there's nothing I enjoy more than cooking for my family?" Destiny explained.

"Well, it's all wonderful," Melanie told her honestly. "I'm impressed."

"It's nothing, really," Destiny said, but she looked pleased, probably because she wasn't used to getting a lot of compliments from the nephews who took her cooking skills for granted.

"Can we stop talking about the food and get to the good stuff?" Mack pleaded, sounding as if he were at least twenty years younger.

Destiny gave him an indulgent smile. "What are you hoping to find under the tree, Mack? They were fresh out of bachelorettes where I shopped."

"How about the keys to a new Jaguar?" he asked hopefully.

"Dream on, little brother," Richard said. "You'll be lucky if you get ashes and switches this year. We all know how badly you've misbehaved."

"I could find you a dozen women who are grateful for that," Mack retorted.

Destiny laughed. "Oh, I managed to do a little better than ashes and switches." She smiled at Melanie. "Even at this age, they're little better than greedy hooligans on Christmas morning. I don't know how I failed them."

"You didn't fail us," Richard assured her. "You taught us the joy of giving…" He paused, then added with a grin, "And receiving."

When Melanie spotted the mound of gifts under the tree, she knew he hadn't been kidding. To her amusement, the three men began tossing the boxes around until there was a little pile beside everyone there, including her. She added her own gifts to their piles, then watched as they tore through paper with an eagerness she would never in a million years have expected from this sophisticated family.

When Richard realized she hadn't opened the first gift, he nudged her. "Hey, you need to get started." He plucked a small box from the pile beside her. "How about this one?"

Melanie took note of the inept wrapping job and concluded it was from him. Something about the size of the box made her decidedly nervous. She made a great show of shaking it, then slowly removing the paper as the others watched and waited expectantly.

When she saw the velvet jeweler's box, her heart skipped, then lurched into a frantic beat. "You didn't," she whispered, her gaze on Richard.

"Open it," he commanded gently. "Please."

Inside, she found a diamond the size of a small boulder. Melanie stared at it in shock.

Ever since their phone conversation a week earlier and the hints he'd subsequently dropped, she had been expecting Richard to do something to catch her completely off guard, but she'd never anticipated anything like this.

She gulped, then looked into all those happy, expectant faces. She couldn't do this. She just couldn't.

Before she could think about it, she dropped the ring, jumped up and ran from the room.

Richard found her outside, taking great gulps of icy air. "Are you okay?" he asked worriedly.

"No, I'm not okay," she replied, her voice shaky. "What were you thinking?"

"That this would be the perfect time to convince Destiny that we're serious."

"You should have warned me."

He sighed. "In retrospect, I should have." He studied her intently. "You really weren't expecting an engagement ring? Not even after all the hints I dropped?"

She shook her head.

"Think you can put this on and go back in there and fake being deliriously happy?" he asked, holding out the ring.

Melanie backed away, hands clasped behind her back. "Even if I were willing to agree to a phony engagement, which I'm not certain I am, I can't wear that.''

''Of course you can.''

''What if I lose it? What if it gets stolen?'' she asked.

Richard shrugged. ''It's insured. Besides, we need a ring like this for the engagement to be convincing.''

Melanie regarded him with dismay. ''You never struck me as the type to go for ostentatious jewelry.''

''I don't. Destiny does.''

''Are you sure about that? She strikes me as a very classy woman.''

''She is, but a ring like this will definitely get her attention.''

She lifted her gaze to his. ''Richard, I'm not sure how much more of this I can take,'' she said honestly.

''I know. Just think of the satisfaction you'll feel when you get to throw this back in my face. I'll probably end up with a black eye or a bloody nose.''

Vaguely cheered by that prospect, she nodded slowly. ''Okay, then. I'll wear the ring.'' She let him put the monstrosity on, then hefted her hand in the air and studied it. ''It's a good thing this is just a game.''

''Isn't it, though?''

But even as he said it, Melanie thought there was an odd expression of regret in Richard's eyes. It made her see something in Richard she'd never expected to see…vulnerability. It reminded her of something Mack had said to her back at the beginning of this farce, that Richard needed someone who could see past his defenses. Now that she had, she realized that was even more dangerous than anything that had happened between them up until now.

Chapter Twelve

Richard stared at Destiny and Melanie huddled together in a corner and concluded that his aunt had bought the phony engagement hook, line and sinker. He was surprised by how guilty that made him feel. He forced himself to examine why that was, but the answer was fairly obvious. He'd never before gone to such elaborate lengths to get even with Destiny for meddling. Usually he just took her interference as a fact of life, something she did out of love—annoying but essentially harmless. He had no idea why he'd felt compelled to go to such an extreme this time. He had a feeling it had a lot to do with his conflicted feelings for Melanie herself.

"Guilty conscience?" Mack inquired, regarding him with amusement.

"I don't want to talk about it," Richard said, not

in the mood to share his soul-searching, even with his brother.

Mack shrugged. "Fine with me, though if you were to ask, I could probably help you sort through all these pesky emotions you're feeling about now."

"When did you turn sensitive?"

"Scoff if you like, but I have more experience in this area than you do, big brother. I have shaded the truth on more than one occasion to evade Destiny's scheming. I'm not especially proud of it, but sometimes I've found it to be a necessity."

"No question about it," Richard said. "I'm just not sure that's a plus."

Mack gave him a knowing look. "You actually believe Destiny is buying all this, don't you?"

Richard was stunned by the suggestion that Destiny wasn't being taken in. "Of course. Just look at her. She's practically gloating at having won so easily."

"Ha!"

Richard frowned at his brother. "What the hell are you suggesting?"

"That our beloved aunt still has the upper hand, that she knows exactly what you're up to and that she is playing along till you dig yourself in so deep you'll never get out. Trust me, this engagement will be real before all is said and done. Destiny will see to it. She's a pro, my friend, and you are a rank amateur when it comes to this kind of scheming."

"You can't be serious," Richard said, even though it made a convoluted kind of sense. Destiny was sneaky enough to do something like that, to give him and Melanie enough rope to hang themselves or, more precisely, to tie themselves together permanently.

"Have you figured out a way to extricate yourself

from this once things get out of hand?'' Mack inquired.

Richard nodded, his gaze now riveted on the two women across the room. What the devil were they talking about? For all he knew the two of them were in cahoots, plotting against him. Maybe Melanie had been in on the scheme from the beginning, Destiny's scheme that is, not his. Good God, he couldn't even keep the schemes straight anymore. Mack was right. He needed a well-formulated escape plan. Fortunately he'd considered that.

''Of course I have a plan,'' he told Mack. ''You know I never go into anything unless I have an exit strategy.''

Mack rolled his eyes. ''This isn't a business deal.''

''Yes, it is,'' Richard said, then felt ridiculous. ''Okay, in a way, it is. Melanie and I have an agreement.''

''In writing?''

''Of course not.''

''So if she changes her mind and decides she likes being engaged to you, that she wants to be married to you, you're prepared for that? Or do you have lawyers on standby ready to break this verbal contract the two of you have?''

''Yes,'' Richard said, then decided that wasn't an admission he was prepared to deal with. ''I mean no. No lawyers. Mack, you're making my head hurt. This is a straightforward arrangement. Melanie and I give Destiny what she wants, proof that we're together—''

''It's an illusion,'' Mach reminded him.

Richard scowled and kept talking. ''Then we break up. I mope around for a while until Destiny finds some other poor woman to try to foist off on me.''

He grinned at Mack. "Or until she decides you're the better candidate for serious romance."

Mack shuddered. "Bite your tongue."

Richard warmed to that scenario. "Yes, indeed. I think that's the way it'll go. She'll be furious that I've messed this up, decide I'm totally hopeless, then give up on me. She'll turn to you, then Ben. Given Ben's current attitude toward the opposite sex, I'll be a doddering old man before she gets back to me again."

"You are so delusional," Mack said. "Even Ben sees Destiny's scheming more clearly than you do and he's oblivious to most of her flaws. He was still laughing his head off when he left here."

That caught Richard's attention. "Ben's gone? When did he leave?"

"Ten, fifteen minutes ago. He slipped out as soon as Destiny's attention was otherwise engaged." He laughed uproariously at his own pun.

Richard was not nearly as amused. He was also worried about his brother. "Why didn't you try to stop him from leaving?"

"Have you ever tried to stop Ben from doing whatever he's set his mind on?" Mack asked. "He's the most stubborn of all of us, and that's saying something. Lighten up. He came today and he actually let down his guard for a while with Melanie."

Richard wasn't comforted by the positive spin. "I hate that he's exiled himself to that isolated farm of his."

Mack sighed. "He needs time, Richard. What happened with Graciela nearly destroyed him."

Richard frowned. "It wasn't his fault."

"He blames himself anyway."

"He needs to listen to reason," Richard said impatiently. "You've told him that. I've told him that. I'm sure Destiny has repeated it ad nauseam. Maybe I should have another talk with him."

"No," Mack said with surprising vehemence. "Destiny's right about this one. Ben needs to heal at his own pace. He doesn't have your thick skin or my cavalier attitude toward life. One day he'll wake up and put the entire tragedy into perspective, but it won't happen until he's ready. If we push him, he'll just dig his heels in deeper. Next thing we know, he'll put a lock on the front gate out there and refuse to let any of us in."

Richard knew Mack was right, but his heart still ached for Ben. Graciela Lofton hadn't been worth all this pain and anguish. No woman was, he thought until he caught a glimpse of Melanie laughing at something Destiny had said. He found himself sighing.

Maybe one woman was worth it, he conceded. Melanie was smarter than he'd initially given her credit for being, sexier than hell and a good sport. It was an admirable combination, one he hadn't run into often.

So why the hell was he so dead set on pushing her out of his life just to make some elaborate point with Destiny?

For a few hours Melanie allowed herself to get caught up in the fantasy. She couldn't seem to tear her gaze away from the disgustingly ostentatious ring that Richard had slipped on her finger. A part of her actually felt this awful kind of letdown that it was only there temporarily.

Not that she wanted this particular ring, not that she even wanted to be engaged to Richard for real, she told herself staunchly, but it would be nice to have that kind of permanent connection to somebody. To know that he'd be there for her in a crisis, to fall asleep in his arms, to make love to. When was the last time she'd had that? During her ill-fated affair with yet another boss and the closeness then had been as much of an illusion as her supposed engagement to Richard was. She sighed heavily, drawing Richard's attention.

"Are you okay?" Richard asked, glancing at her quickly as he drove toward her place.

"Just tired," she said. "Trying to keep all the threads of our story straight wore me out."

He nodded, his jaw tight. "I can relate to that."

"How? You spent most of the afternoon huddled with Mack. He knows we're lying. I was with Destiny, who had a million and one questions about our plans."

"What did you tell her?"

"That you caught me completely off guard today, that we have no plans."

"Sounds reasonable. What was so tricky about that?"

She gave him a withering look. "Are you kidding? Ever heard about nature abhorring a vacuum? Well, Destiny has nothing on nature. She now has lists of her lists."

"Lists?" Richard echoed, his expression dire. "Oh, God."

She grinned despite her own trepidations. "I see you're familiar with her list-making skills. Frankly, I was in awe, and I consider myself to be a halfway decent organizer."

"What sort of lists was she making?" Richard asked warily.

"Guest lists, caterers, florists, photographers, bridal salons, gift registries. I believe there is also a short list of preferable wedding dates to be checked first thing in the morning with your church. I lost track after that one." She gave him a plaintive look. "She wants to book the church. Isn't it some kind of sin to book a church for a wedding you know will never take place?"

Richard forced a grim laugh. "Probably not a sin, but definitely a complication we could live without. You haven't met our minister. He would not be amused."

"Oh, and did I mention Destiny has also drafted the engagement announcement for your approval, though I wouldn't count on her waiting? She seems a bit eager to get it into print."

"Maybe Mack is right," Richard muttered under his breath, his gloomy expression deepening.

"What?"

"Mack," he said. "He thinks she's on to us and is now determined to push us beyond the brink so there will be no turning back."

"It wouldn't surprise me," Melanie said glumly. She regarded him hopefully. "When can we break up?"

Richard didn't respond. He merely pulled the car to a stop at the side of the road and set the brake.

"Richard? Did you hear me?"

"I heard you."

"Well?"

"Give me a minute. I need to think about it."

Melanie wasn't about to give him a minute. She

wanted a solution and she wanted it now. "This plan is backfiring on us, isn't it?"

"Could be."

"Then fix it, dammit."

He gave her an enigmatic look. "Any suggestions?"

"Tell her the truth," Melanie said impatiently. "How's that for a novel idea?"

"I'm not even sure I know what the truth is anymore," he admitted, his expression oddly wistful.

"I'll tell you what the truth is. We are not engaged!" she said, her voice rising.

"You're wearing my ring," he reminded her mildly.

"It's fake."

"I can assure you it's not."

She scowled at him. "I mean it doesn't mean anything. The engagement is a fraud, a hoax, a stupid game."

"It definitely started that way," Richard agreed.

Something in his tone stopped her from continuing her own ranting. "Richard?"

He lifted his gaze to hers, his eyes troubled. Then, before she could guess his intention, he leaned across and touched his lips to hers, softly, tenderly. Heat flared as if he'd touched a match to kindling.

They sat by the side of the road, the motor idling, oblivious to the passing traffic, caught up in a kiss that shook Melanie to her very core. She wanted to cling to him, to keep his mouth against hers forever, to taste him, to let that heat build and build until there wasn't a thought left in her head, until she was only feeling these intense, wicked sensations that he stirred in her.

She hadn't bargained for this, had told herself a million times not to get involved, not to let down her guard for even an instant. All good resolutions. All wasted. She was involved. She was in love.

She was doomed.

Even knowing that—heaven help her—she couldn't seem to stop kissing him. Richard was the one who finally backed away, looking as shattered as she felt. A small, annoying smile tugged at his lips.

"What?" she grumbled.

"That kiss felt damn real to me," he said.

"It can't be," she protested, still trying to cling to some tiny shred of sanity.

"Who says?"

"I do. We agreed—"

He shrugged, still looking vaguely amused. "Things change."

"But they haven't changed," she insisted vehemently. "I won't let them change. I can't."

He blinked at her fierce tone. "Why?"

"I work for you, dammit. I told you I will not be put in that position again."

He nodded slowly, his expression suddenly shuttered. "So you did."

His easy acceptance of that should have filled her with relief. It didn't.

"Please take me home," she requested quietly.

"No problem."

Trying to put some professional distance between them, she asked, "Are we going to meet with the finalists for your campaign manager's job this week?"

He shook his head. "I'm having Winifred postpone that."

She gave him a sharp look. "Why?"

"Let's just say I'm reexamining my priorities."

She stared at him blankly. "What does that mean?"

"I'll let you know when I figure it out."

Melanie was still pondering Richard's enigmatic remark when Destiny called first thing in the morning a few days after Christmas.

"Richard tells me he's given you the day off," she said cheerily.

"I have other clients," Melanie reminded her.

"No one works during the holidays."

Melanie couldn't deny that. Her phone had been silent for several days now. Even Becky was off at the holiday sales, a ritual she engaged in with the fervor of a true shopaholic.

"I was hoping to catch up on a few things while the office is quiet," Melanie claimed. What she did not want to do was spend time trying to come up with more believable fibs to feed to Destiny. She felt crummy enough about the growing pile of lies as it was.

"Whatever you're doing can wait," Destiny said. "I have other plans." Her tone suggested Melanie was expected to fall in with them without question.

"What?" Melanie asked suspiciously, visions of all those lists still haunting her.

"Just a little preliminary scouting expedition," Destiny said cheerfully. "It'll be fun."

"You want to go shopping today? I'd rather eat dirt."

"We'll start with lunch and champagne. That should get you into the proper spirit," Destiny said, undaunted by Melanie's lack of enthusiasm. "I'll pick you up in an hour. Wear comfortable shoes."

She hung up before Melanie could come up with one single protest that Destiny would buy.

Even though she dreaded the entire outing, Melanie quickly got swept along on Destiny's tide of excitement. She tried reminding herself that her enjoyment of Destiny's exuberance was what had gotten her into this predicament with Richard in the first place, but that didn't seem to work as well as she'd hoped. The woman's high spirits were contagious.

Before Melanie knew it, she was caught up in the whole shopping thing. She told herself it wouldn't hurt, just this once, to try on a few wedding gowns in some of the most exclusive shops around. Who knew when she might have another chance to indulge in such a fantasy? As long as she didn't sign a single credit-card slip or exit a shop with a package, what was the harm?

Her delusion lasted for about the space of a heart-beat. Within no time the shopping excursion began spinning wildly out of her control. Destiny on a mission was a force to be reckoned with. She knew the owners of every elegant boutique in Old Town Alexandria, Georgetown, and in the fanciest malls in the region. She was an indefatigable shopper.

She also knew her own mind and had little patience for salesclerks who wasted time showing them anything less than the best. Despite the brakes Melanie tried valiantly to put on, Destiny merely waved off her objections and headed for the next store. Short of planting her heels and making the woman drag her along behind, Melanie was at a loss. Her vow not to use her credit card for a single purchase was never once tested. Destiny wielded hers with the skill of a woman for whom money held no meaning beyond its purchasing power.

"I can't let you do this," Melanie uttered more times than she could count. She was wasting her breath. The packages kept piling up. The only conceivable thing that might slow Destiny down would be running out of trunk space, Melanie thought hopefully as she tried to cram one more package into the already jammed trunk.

"Looks like that's it for the day," she said a bit too enthusiastically. "We're out of room."

"Nonsense. We'll just have everything else sent," Destiny said, turning to march off to the next store on her exhaustive list.

"You can't be serious," Melanie said. "I'm wiped out."

"Really?" Destiny regarded her with surprise. "I'm just getting my second wind, but if you're tired, I'll take you home." She beamed. "I can't tell you when I've had such a wonderful time. What time should we get started tomorrow? Another day or two like this one and we'll have made real inroads."

"In what? Bolstering the national economy?"

Destiny laughed. "That, too. Is ten o'clock good for you?"

Melanie ran through a frantic litany of excuses. Alone, none of them seemed to do the trick, but combined they finally bought her the next day off.

"The day after then," Destiny said adamantly, obviously not inclined to be put off a second time. "I'll pick you up at nine. We'll start with florists and caterers, then do a bit more shopping."

Melanie felt her stomach start to churn. "I can't let you do all this. It's wrong."

"I'm enjoying every minute of it."

She was, too. Melanie could see it in her eyes and that made her feel even guiltier. Panicked that the frenzy would only get worse, the second Destiny had gone, she got into her own car and drove to Richard's office. He was bound to be there. She hauled along a few packages—the veritable tip of the iceberg—to help her make her point.

Richard glanced up when she came charging in under a full head of steam. His gaze narrowed. "I wasn't expecting to see you today."

"Yes, well, the day is full of surprises. I wasn't expecting this, either." She dumped the packages on his desk. It made the piles on Christmas morning seem a little sparse. "Look what she's done," she moaned.

"Destiny?" he guessed as if there might be some other crazed shopper in the family.

"Who else?" she snapped. "She picked out china and silver, bought my veil—it's hand-tatted French lace, by the way—and started on my trousseau. She would not take no for an answer. She said I have a position to live up to as your fiancée. She wouldn't let me pay for a thing, not that I could afford to pay for one sterling-silver place setting, much less the twelve she ordered. We have to stop this, Richard. It's getting out of hand. No, it's beyond that. It's completely crazy. Destiny had the time of her life and I feel like the lowest slug on the planet."

Even as she ranted, he reached into a bag and pulled out a silky negligee. His eyes immediately filled with heat.

"Yes, I can see that," he murmured.

It was said in a placating tone she found totally annoying. Nor did he look nearly as distressed as Melanie had anticipated. "Richard, are you hearing what I'm saying? This has to stop. She's spending a fortune on a wedding that is not going to take place. She's out of control. This whole mess is out of control."

"I hear you." He held up the negligee, that hot gleam still in his eyes. "This doesn't have to go to waste, though, does it?"

She stared at him. "What?"

His gaze caught hers. "It would be a shame to let this go to waste, don't you think?"

Her pulse raced. "Are you crazy?" she asked, her voice a little too breathless. Surely he wasn't suggesting…

"Come away with me," he said, "Please."

"I don't think—"

He smiled. "There you go. Don't think. I've spent the whole day doing enough thinking for both of us. Just say yes, Melanie. We'll go down to the cottage for a few days."

"So we can figure out how to handle this?" she said, still trying to maintain the illusion that that gleam in his eyes did not mean what she thought it meant—okay, what she *wanted* it to mean.

His smile spread. "That's one reason."

She regarded him suspiciously. "What's the other one?"

"So I can see you wearing this," he said quietly, letting the filmy material run through his fingers. He met her gaze again. "And take it off of you."

Oh, God, she thought, her heart hammering.

"Well?"

In her head, she heard herself saying no. It was loud, clear and decisive. She repeated it just to be sure.

Then she looked into Richard's expectant gaze.

"Yes," she whispered.

Apparently she wasn't satisfied that her life hadn't descended into total heartbreak yet. She was determined to careen wildly straight into disaster.

Chapter Thirteen

Though Richard had spent the entire day trying to figure out the best way to handle things with Melanie and Destiny, he hadn't come to any satisfactory conclusions by the time Melanie had come bursting into his office twenty minutes earlier. Leaning back in his chair, listening to Melanie's outpouring of dismay over their duplicity, watching the color rise in her cheeks, hearing the passion in her voice had convinced him of one thing. He wasn't going to let her go the way he'd originally intended.

To the contrary, in fact. He was going to do his best to figure out some way to keep her in his life. After all the scheming, he realized he might have a teensy bit of trouble getting her to trust him, but he'd overcome tougher obstacles in his life.

He might still be more than a little miffed over his aunt's meddling, but Destiny had gotten it right. Melanie was exactly what he'd needed. He should have known Destiny wouldn't make a mistake with his happiness on the line. No one on earth knew him better, flaws and all. She'd found a woman capable of balancing his natural stodginess, a woman who could make him feel alive, a woman whose passion would make him lose his head and his heart...if only he dared to risk them.

As he'd listened to Melanie, he'd realized that for him all bets were off. Unfortunately, he'd made a commitment to her that she could end their phony relationship. He'd realized that he had one chance— if he was lucky—to convince her that ending things wasn't what she wanted, either.

For a man not normally inclined to risk rejection, he'd taken a huge chance by inviting her down to the cottage. Letting her know that he had more than talking on his mind had been an even bigger risk, but he couldn't deceive her about his intentions. He might take all the well-intentioned lies to Destiny reasonably lightly, but he would not lie to Melanie. They had enough hurdles to get over without adding that.

Looking across his desk at her now, heat in her cheeks, her eyes bright, he knew he would do whatever was necessary to persuade her to stay with him forever. Never before had he allowed anyone to begin to matter so much. The power of his feelings for her very nearly overwhelmed him.

"Are you sure about this?" he asked. "Do you really want to go to the cottage with me?"

She nodded.

"You know I'm asking you there to do more than talk."

A smile played on her lips as she gestured toward

that breathtaking concoction of deep blue silk and lace. "You made that clear."

"Your employment as a consultant to my campaign has nothing at all to do with this," he said to make sure she understood that. "Your work here is secure, no matter what happens between us personally. I'll put that in writing if you like."

"No need," she said. "I quit."

Richard blinked, certain he couldn't possibly have heard her correctly. "What?"

"I said I quit," she repeated more confidently. "I don't need your business."

Now there was a wrinkle he hadn't anticipated. He'd counted on that tie keeping her around, even if he messed up something this week. It had been his sketchily formed backup plan.

"But I want you to go on working for me," he said, surprised to find that he meant every word of it and not just because it had been his fall-back plan for contact with her. Damn, if it wasn't one more thing he owed Destiny for. He regarded Melanie intently. "You're too good to lose. I read your notes on the prospective campaign managers. They were sharp and insightful. You got a far better fix on their qualifications than I did by looking at the exact same material."

Satisfaction glowed in her eyes. "Then I'll be happy to bill you for that, but I still quit."

"Why?"

"It will just muddy the waters. I don't know where this trip to the cottage will lead, but I do know that I don't want to be worrying about whether I'll have a job when things end between us. And, frankly, it would be far too painful for me to be around you, when things do go badly.''

When, not *if.* She'd said it twice. Richard heard her certainty that the relationship would end and wondered what it would take to convince her otherwise.

In the meantime, he had to find some way to keep her from quitting. He needed all his ties with her to be strong. To his astonishment, he'd gotten used to having her underfoot. He didn't want to lose any aspect of that. He didn't want to lose yet another important person in his life. Losing his parents had shaped his entire outlook. He didn't think he'd survive another emotional hit like that.

''I thought this consulting job was going to be your big break,'' he reminded her, grasping desperately at straws. ''That's what Destiny led me to believe. Was she wrong?''

''No, she wasn't wrong.'' Her gaze remained unflinching. ''I'll find another big break, Richard, one without the complications.''

Richard heard the finality in her voice and nodded slowly, not even trying to hide his reluctance to let this be the last word on the subject. ''You're sure?''

She chuckled. ''As sure as I've been about anything since the day we met. Things have been a bit confusing since then.''

''Tell me about it,'' he responded.

''Maybe you're the one who needs to think about this trip you have planned. Are you sure? You're not a man who's big on complications, and this could be a huge one.''

Richard grinned at her assessment. It had been true once, not all that long ago. He'd hated sticky situations, especially of a personal nature. But he was definitely looking forward to this one. For the first time ever he saw the possibility of a real future for a relationship, something more than satisfying sex.

He stood up and walked around his desk to stand in front of her. "I'm sure about this one," he said with quiet assurance. "I don't know how it happened, but I can't get you out of my head."

Her gaze narrowed suspiciously. "Are you hoping this weekend will purge me from your system? Because if that's the case, let's call the whole thing off. We can forget about the trip, the phony engagement, all of it. I'll return all this stuff and take all the blame with Destiny."

The possibility that she could turn her back on him so easily grated. Richard looked directly into her eyes. "I appreciate the offer, but that's not how it's going to happen."

She bristled visibly at his tone. "Oh?" she asked, as if daring him to utter another order.

"Here's what we're going to do. We're going to the cottage. We're going to put all of this other nonsense aside for the next few days. We're going to make love until we're exhausted, then maybe do it a few more times just to be sure we're getting it right."

"Were you an activities director at one of those singles resorts in another life?"

Richard chuckled at the totally incongruous suggestion. "I seriously doubt it. Are we clear about the plans?"

For a minute he seriously thought she might balk, but she finally met his gaze.

"Okay," she said quietly but firmly. There was no apparent doubt in her eyes or in her tone.

His heart soared. So did his libido. He was wise

enough not to let her know about either reaction. "Good, then. I'll pick you up in an hour."

"We're going tonight?"

"No time like the present. My desk is clear. Yours?"

"Clear enough," she admitted. "I have plans with Destiny day after tomorrow."

"I'll take care of that. I'll tell her we're going on a romantic getaway before all the wedding frenzy takes over our lives. She'll be delighted."

"Maybe you can convince her not to do anything precipitous without us," Melanie suggested hopefully. "Tell her we want to be a part of every decision. That way there's a slight chance we won't come back and find that every detail has been hammered out and nailed down with ironclad contracts."

Richard nodded at the sensible suggestion. "Good idea. I'll call now. You'd better get moving if you intend to be ready in an hour."

She gave him a long, measuring look, then scooped up the negligee that made his mouth go dry, let it dangle sexily from a finger, and said, "How much packing will I need to do, if this is all you expect me to wear?"

Richard was still trying to form a coherent thought when she sashayed past him. Given that remark, he wondered if it was possible they could be on the road in thirty minutes. Of course, with his body in a state of complete and total arousal, it might be very wise not to leave his office for a while.

Melanie arrived back at her house to find Becky sitting at her desk, staring glumly at her computer screen.

"What are you doing here?"

"I came in because I needed to talk to a friend. Where were you?" she asked accusingly. "You told me you'd be working today."

"Long story," Melanie said, regarding Becky with concern, her own plans forgotten for the moment. "What's wrong? They were all out of your size at Nordstrom's?"

"I didn't go shopping."

That was so startling Melanie sank down in her own chair. "Why not?"

"I broke up with Jason."

"Again? Why?"

"He's been cheating on me."

All of Melanie's good feelings toward the man vanished at once. "How did you find out? Are you sure?" she asked, sharing Becky's indignation.

"I spotted him with a woman in the men's department," Becky said. "Trust me, I recognized all the signs. She was practically drooling over him." She regarded Melanie with obvious misery. "And that was after he'd told me he'd rather be carved up into itty-bitty pieces than go shopping right after Christmas. He *knew* where I was going. He *wanted* me to see them together. The coward. It was easier than being honest with me."

"You're right. It was a cowardly thing to do," Melanie agreed. "But, Becky, wouldn't you rather know the truth?"

"No," Becky said at once, then sighed. "Okay, yes, but it's the holiday season. Who will I be with on New Year's Eve?" She regarded Melanie hopefully. "We could do something. There's still time to plan a party."

Melanie debated telling Richard they would have to be back for New Year's Eve, then decided against it. They had their own problems to sort through.

"I can't."

"You have a date?"

"In a way. Richard and I are going away."

Becky's mouth dropped open, her own sad plight momentarily forgotten. "You're kidding! Where? When?"

"We're going back to the cottage at the beach." She glanced at her watch. "In about twenty minutes. I need to pack."

"Then go. Don't worry about me."

Melanie hesitated. It didn't seem right to abandon her friend now. "Will you be all right?"

Becky gave her a brave smile. "Aren't I always? It's not like this will be the first New Year's Eve I've ever spent alone."

"Don't spend it alone," Melanie urged her. "Promise me you'll call someone, go out to dinner, go to a movie, something. Do not stay at home and cry over Jason the jerk."

Becky squared her shoulders. "Don't worry. I've shed my last tears over him." Her expression brightened. "In fact, I think I'll go home right now and take a pair of scissors to all those expensive designer shirts of his."

"There you go," Melanie said. "He deserves that and more."

Becky's good mood promptly deflated. "Of course, that's probably just what he expects me to do. That's probably one more reason he was buying shirts on sale today."

"Doesn't matter," Melanie said. "You'll still feel

better once you've savored a little revenge. Just remember how he loves his wardrobe. I always thought there was something a little weird about that. The man spent more on clothes than we do.''

Becky yanked open a drawer in her desk and pulled out a pair of lethal-looking scissors. ''These are sharper than the ones I have at home,'' she said gleefully as she tucked them into her purse.

''Have fun,'' Melanie called after her.

Becky was barely out the door when Richard came in.

''You're not ready,'' he guessed after surveying the room for any evidence of a suitcase.

''Sorry. We had a crisis around here.''

''I assume that's why Becky went charging past me with a somewhat maniacal glint in her eyes.''

Melanie grinned. ''She's on the warpath.''

''Boyfriend?''

''Ex-boyfriend.''

''His life's not in danger, is it?''

''Nope. Just his wardrobe.''

Richard chuckled. ''Remind me never to make you angry.''

Melanie patted his cheek. ''You make me furious all the time,'' she reminded him. ''So far, though, your clothes are safe.''

''Too bad. I was rather looking forward to having you rip them off of me.''

Melanie gave him a considering look. ''An interesting idea. I'll give it some thought on the way to the cottage.''

''Don't think out loud,'' he warned. ''I'd hate to have to stop at one of those less-than-stellar motels on the way down.''

"No chance of that. I'm going to be enjoying testing your patience too much."

Richard's patience was hanging by a thread by the time they finally got to the cottage. If there was any clothes ripping to be done, he was likely to be the one doing it. He was still a bit surprised that his restraint was as strong as it evidently was.

"Do you want me to make a fire?" he asked when they'd carried everything inside, including several bags of gourmet food he'd brought from home and their luggage. For the first time in recent memory, his laptop computer wasn't among the possessions he'd brought along. A rather impressive, unopened box of condoms was.

Melanie met his gaze. "A fire would be romantic," she said, then grinned. "But it would take too long. Maybe later."

"Dinner?" he asked, his voice oddly choked.

She took a step closer, letting her coat fall from her shoulders into a heap on the floor. "Later."

"Wine?"

She shook her head, her gaze locked with his. "Uh-uh. I'm already a little giddy." She reached for the top button on his shirt. "You're a little too prim and proper for the setting."

His gaze narrowed. "Are you really sure you want to start this right here, right now?"

"Oh, yeah," she said fervently.

"I haven't even turned the heat up."

"We won't need it," she said confidently.

He grinned finally. "Well, then, I guess one of us has her priorities all sorted out."

"For the short term," she agreed.

The phrase hit Richard like a slap, reminding him that he was treading on very thin ice. Neither of them had said a thing about permanency. This was an experiment, at least in her eyes. He'd done nothing to suggest otherwise.

"Then let's make it memorable," he said, pulling her into his arms and settling his mouth on hers.

This time there was no holding back. There was nothing tentative or uncertain or exploratory about the kiss. They both already knew that a kiss had the power to stir them.

Melanie was restless in his embrace when he scooped her up and headed for the stairs.

"Where are we going?" she murmured against his lips.

"To bed," he told her. "I can forget about the fire, the food and the wine, but I am not going to make love to you for the first time in the middle of the living room floor."

She grinned. "Afraid of a little rug burn?"

He heard the laughing challenge in her voice. "No, just determined to treat you the way you deserve to be treated."

Her eyes turned dreamy. "Sometimes you say the sweetest things."

"Sometimes you inspire me," he admitted as he strode into his bedroom. It was like an icebox, making him regret his decision not to bother just yet with turning up the heat. "I really think I should run back downstairs and kick up the furnace."

Melanie slid her hand inside his shirt, then slipped lower till her fingers were grazing the bare skin just below his waist. "Still cold?" she inquired.

"As a matter of fact," he began, only to moan as

her deft fingers slipped a little lower. "Okay, now I'm hot."

"Told you," she said gleefully.

He met her gaze, his expression suddenly serious. "Do you have any idea how much I've thought about this?"

"You think too much," she responded, still exploring his body in a way she had to know was likely to drive him mad.

Richard swallowed hard, trying to maintain some control. "In other words, you'd prefer action?"

"At the moment, most definitely."

He nodded. "Okay, then. I was taught to always defer to a lady's wishes, at least in a situation like this."

"Who taught you that? Destiny?"

"No, Mack. He has a very successful track record."

"What did Destiny tell you when she taught you about the birds and the bees?"

"That sex is always better when you're in love," he said quietly, his gaze on her face.

Melanie's eyes filled with an emotion he couldn't quite fathom. He was getting better at reading her, but this was something new. Something tender. It gave him hope.

He wasn't certain enough of his footing here, though, to say the rest of what was in his heart, that this was the very first time he'd put that theory about sex and love to the test.

The game had just taken a serious turn. Melanie felt the shift somewhere deep inside and it terrified her. She'd come down here because she'd lost the last shred of willpower and sense she possessed. She wanted whatever this trip would bring. She wanted memories to savor and cling to on the lonely nights in the future when Richard was out of her life again.

That day would come eventually. She had no doubts about that. He was obviously attracted to her, but chemistry was a transitory thing. Eventually he'd remember that she drove him nuts and they would stage their breakup. That would be that. It was what they'd agreed to, and Richard was known for not going back on his word. It was one of his most admirable qualities. Even her own preliminary press releases said so.

At least the certainty of a breakup was what she'd been counting on until about five seconds ago, when the look in Richard's eyes had been so filled with heat and emotion that it had shaken her. Until now she'd had very little at stake. In fact, she'd believed the only real thing she could lose was an important consulting contract, which was why she'd tossed that aside earlier. It no longer complicated matters, and recent weeks had proved to her that her professional ideas and strategies had real worth. She would find other clients. She'd felt relieved the minute she'd quit the consulting job.

Now it was all personal. It all mattered. This heat between them, the growing respect they had for each other, her delight in Destiny and the rest of Richard's family—all that had caught her off guard. She was flat out in love with Richard, but she'd learned once before that she couldn't trust herself to accurately assess what a man was feeling. She'd been burned too badly last time.

Play it light. Pretend none of it matters. Those were

the lessons she'd learned in her last disastrous relationship. She had to remember that now. She had to protect her heart at all costs. Until and unless Richard said something about calling off their fake engagement, until he suggested making it real instead, she had to operate under the belief that nothing had changed beyond their admission that the attraction between them was too hot to ignore.

"Why so serious?" he asked, his voice low, his gaze intense.

"I just got lost in thought for a minute," she said. She forced an impish grin. "Where were we?"

He took her hand, kissed the palm, then placed it low on his belly. "Right about here, as I recall." He gazed deep into her eyes. "And wandering."

"Ah, yes," she said, giving herself up to sensation again, thrilling to each touch she initiated, loving that he seemed willing to let her be in charge.

Richard's gasp was audible when she ventured further, discovering his body in all its masculine splendor. A glint in his eyes, he suddenly flipped her on her back and began deftly undoing buttons and snaps, until she was naked beneath him. The shift in power left her breathless and wanting more.

"Let me see if I understand the agenda you have in mind," he said, slowly working his way down her body.

Slow, exploratory caresses were followed by long, lingering kisses until she was writhing restlessly. There was definitely no need for external heat now. She was on fire from the inside out, a demanding, relentless fire that only he could quench. She could lose herself in flames like this.

"How long do you plan on tormenting me?" she

asked, wanting him buried inside her, needing that connection, that fullness as his body stretched hers.

"A bit longer," he said with another teasing stroke that was almost her undoing. "Let it go, Melanie."

She shook her head, stubborn even at a moment like this. "Not without you."

His gaze stayed on her face. "Please," he said quietly, touching her intimately, tormenting her until control was out of question.

It was the quiet plea that did it. Spasms rocked through her, delicious, unexpected sensations that should have satisfied, but made her crave more.

His look was smug, too smug. It drove her to drastic measures.

"You don't get to control everything," she said, fighting a grin as she executed a move she'd learned in a self-defense class that had Richard under her, shock in his eyes. The move wasn't quite as smooth as it had been in class, but it got the job done.

"Where the devil did you learn to do that?" he asked.

"Doesn't matter. It's just important that you know that I can do it." She tried to fight a satisfied grin of her own and lost. She'd never expected those time-consuming lessons to pay off in quite this way. "Now, then, tell me what you'd like me to do."

He reached up and captured her face with his hands, then drew her mouth down to his. "This," he murmured against her lips. "Just this."

"That's all?"

"And this."

He lifted her hips, then settled her again, filling her just the way she'd imagined. He held her steady, back in control, his gaze locked with hers. Melanie felt as if they were at war, but if this went the way she expected, they'd both win.

At last, he moved, thrusting up slowly, surely, then withdrawing until she had to bite her lip to keep from pleading with him.

Then there was no more question of control. They were both lost to sensation, slick and hot, hard and demanding, spiraling closer and closer to that elusive release.

When it came at last, it was shattering, leaving her weak and spent and filled with so much emotion she was scared to look into his eyes for fear he would see the truth—that she loved him beyond measure. She wasn't sure it was a truth either of them could live with.

Chapter Fourteen

It was nearly midnight when Richard crept out of bed and went downstairs to turn up the heat. Even with Melanie snuggled close, the frigid air in the room was beginning to penetrate all the way through to his bones.

Tonight had been a revelation. He'd never had a woman give to him so completely, so unselfishly, so enthusiastically. There was no question in his mind that Melanie was after his money or his power. She'd had access to both and had turned them down, seemingly without a backward glance. He believed with all his heart that her feelings were personal, and that was what he'd waited a lifetime to find without even realizing how desperately he wanted it.

So why was he still holding back? Why hadn't he told her what was in *his* heart, even though she hadn't said what was in hers? Was he such a coward that he feared rejection? He hated admitting it, but that was exactly it.

He could go into an election a few months from now and face rejection by the voters without batting an eye, but he was terrified of opening his heart to Melanie, only to discover that she intended to stick by the original rules and walk away. He knew too well what that kind of devastating loss felt like. True, his parents hadn't chosen to die and leave him and his brothers, but the effect had been traumatic just the same. If Melanie *chose* to go, it would be even worse. He knew that a man never completely recovered from a loss like that. His cowardice now was proof of that.

While he was downstairs, he took the food they'd brought with them from its freezer chest and put it into the refrigerator. Thankfully, it was still cold.

Then he flipped on a single light over the counter, brewed a pot of decaf coffee and sat down at the kitchen table to think. He thought about all the times Destiny had told him that he couldn't let his parents' deaths scare him away from love.

"Protecting your heart is self-defeating," she told him on a dark night when he'd awakened from a childhood nightmare in which he'd relived the loss of his parents. "At the end of the day you're just as lonely as if you'd loved and lost."

Richard had nodded his understanding, but the truth was he hadn't believed her. Surely nothing could be as painful as the void left when someone went away forever.

"You believe I love you, don't you?" she'd persisted.

He had nodded again, accepting the truth of that. She had been a steady, solid presence in his life from

the day she'd breezed back from France and said she
intended to stay and take care of him and his brothers.
He trusted her—loved her—as he did few people, but
there was a part of his heart he held back, protected.
Slowly but surely he'd shielded himself from feeling
anything for anyone.

"Are you scared I'll leave? Or that I'll die?"

Unable to voice such a terrible fear aloud, he'd
merely nodded acknowledgment of that, too.

"Oh, sweetie, I will never leave," Destiny had
vowed to him time and again. "It's true that I might
die. We all do one day. But that doesn't mean we
shouldn't love each other. Instead we should be grateful for every minute we have together. Life is meant
to be lived. If I haven't taught you the importance of
seizing the moment, of taking chances, of loving
someone with everything that's in you, then I've
failed you."

She'd tried so valiantly to instill that lesson in
him—in all of them—yet Richard had been resistant.
So had Mack and Ben in their own ways. Mack had
filled his life with meaningless affairs. Ben had loved
well but not wisely, and the pain of that loss had
cemented all of his old fears. Richard wondered if
Ben would ever open his heart again.

Richard had never risked anything at all. Until Melanie had come along, he'd been certain all his determined efforts to protect his heart had been successful.
He'd believed he was completely incapable of real
emotion.

He was on his second cup of coffee and still brooding when he heard Melanie's footsteps on the stairs.
His pulse kicked up in anticipation, oblivious to all

those old fears that had been tormenting him once more in the dark of night.

She wandered into the dimly lit kitchen wearing his shirt and looking sexily rumpled. "I missed you," she said sleepily, crossing the room and snuggling onto his lap in a totally trusting way that made his heart and his body ache.

Richard's arms went around her automatically. Instantly he was all too aware of her bare thighs against his own, of her bare bottom intimately pressed against his boxers. Whatever faint hope he'd held of regaining his equilibrium with her flew out the window.

"I came down to turn up the heat," he murmured against her ear, drinking in the faint scent of perfume that lingered on her skin.

"You should have turned up *my* heat," she said lightly.

He grinned at the saucy suggestion. "Now why didn't I think of that? Is it too late?" He skimmed a caress over her breast, saw the tip bead under the soft cotton of his shirt.

"We might be able to work something out," she teased. "But first you have to feed me. I'm starved."

"So many appetites," he said with amusement. "Are you absolutely certain food is what you want first?"

A gleam lit her eyes as his touch wandered. "You're making it very difficult, but yes. I want sustenance."

"Dinner? Breakfast? A sandwich?"

She moaned. "Don't make me think. I'm half-asleep. Surprise me."

"An intriguing notion," Richard said. "You going

to let me stand up, or am I expected to manage a meal while holding you?''

She stretched—yet another torment—then rose slowly and moved to another chair. She immediately put her tousled head down on her arms on the table. For all Richard could tell, she went straight back to sleep. His gaze seemed to lock on the nape of her neck. He wondered how she would taste there. It was one of the few places he hadn't sampled earlier.

Resisting the urge to find out, he poked his head into the refrigerator instead and retrieved the makings for a chicken and avocado sandwich. He checked the freezer and found a container of Destiny's homemade vegetable soup he could zap in the microwave.

Melanie remained perfectly still as he worked, not twitching so much as a muscle until he put the food down in front of her. Then as if drawn by the spicy scent of the hot soup, she sniffed delicately and lifted her head.

''Oh, my,'' she whispered. ''Tell me this is homemade.''

He laughed. ''It is, but I can't take the credit. Destiny always leaves some in the freezer.''

''It smells heavenly.'' She took a spoonful, blew on it to cool it, then put it in her mouth. ''Tastes heavenly, too.'' Wide-awake now, she glanced at the sandwich. ''Chicken and avocado on a baguette? Very fancy.''

''I will take credit for that,'' he said, amused by her enthusiasm. ''Do you really not cook anything?''

''I'll have you know I've never ruined a frozen dinner.''

''Now there's a culinary claim to be proud of,'' he

said, laughing, his earlier cares forgotten for the moment.

"Fortunately, I am not in your life because of my skill in the kitchen," she said. "If I were, you would be doomed to disappointment."

"You could never disappoint me," he said. Unless she went through with the breakup. That would tear him apart.

She caught his gaze, studied him intently. "You sure about that?" she asked. "You looked kind of funny there for a second, as if there was something you weren't saying."

Now, he thought, now would be the perfect time to open it all up, to tell her that everything had changed. He wanted to do it. He should do it. He even opened his mouth to speak, but in the end, he remained silent, a prisoner to his longstanding doubts and fears.

And as he saw Melanie's expression close down, saw the light in her eyes die at his silence, he knew that he'd lost what might have been his best chance for getting what he wanted for the rest of his life.

Melanie knew that something significant had happened during their late-night meal in the kitchen. She even guessed that Richard had wrestled with his demons and lost, but she had no idea what to do about it. Though she was assertive about so many things in her life, confident of her professional skills, even assured about most of her relationships, she'd lost that self-assurance when it came to matters of the heart.

Truthfully, she had been praying that allowing herself to be open and vulnerable would be enough, that she would never have to actually risk putting her feel-

ings into words that could be thrown back into her
face. She knew the power of words better than anyone. They could heal or wound, but once spoken they
could never be undone.

Not entirely daunted by Richard's silence, she left
herself open to what might transpire between now and
whenever they went back to Alexandria. She could
do that much. She'd come down here hoping for a
chance to make this work. They'd made so much progress, achieved a whole new level of intimacy. It was
too soon to give up on getting more.

In the morning, it seemed that Richard had reached
a similar conclusion. He greeted her with a smile and
a breakfast worthy of a gourmet chef in a country inn.

"You know I might reconsider marrying you for
real if you promised me a meal like this every morning," she teased lightly.

"You've got it," he said just as lightly. "Of
course, we'll both be waddling into the doctor's office
with high cholesterol and high blood pressure before
we hit forty."

She sighed as she took another bite of a fluffy om-
elette made with goat cheese and chives. "It might
be worth it."

He gave her a once-over that told her he appreci-
ated the way she looked right now. "So, what are we
going to do to work off these calories?" he asked, an
unmistakably hopeful note in his voice.

"Not that," she said decisively. She needed to reclaim a bit of distance this morning, gain some perspective on the night before.

"Too bad."

She grinned. "I'll give you a rain check. I want to
go sight-seeing."

He regarded her with surprise. "You do?"

"I glanced through some of those brochures in the living room last time I was here. There's George Washington's birthplace, Robert E. Lee's birthplace, a winery. This could be fun."

"The winery holds a certain appeal. I'm not so sure about the rest. Destiny considered all that history to be part of our summer experience."

"You didn't enjoy it?"

"Maybe I didn't make myself clear," he said. "We went *every* summer."

"Ah." She grinned. "Then we won't need a guide, will we? You can tell me everything."

"I'm pretty sure I've blocked all the details."

"I'll get a book and test you," she responded, refusing to relent. "Now let's get moving."

"Now who's acting like an activities director?" he grumbled, but he did get up and stack the dishes in the dishwasher.

Melanie grinned at his attitude. She patted his cheek. "Don't pout. When we get home you can test me."

"On the history?"

"No, on my responsiveness to other commands."

His expression brightened at that. "Put on your walking shoes, darling. These are going to be lightning-fast tours."

Richard found to his amazement that he could put last night's disappointment and worries behind him and fall in with Melanie's playful mood. She soaked up the history lessons with astonishing attention, making him sift through years of tidbits for the most fascinating ones in his memory. He loved that she listened so intently, her expression as rapt as if he were divulging bits of current gossip about still-living neighbors.

"I know as a Yankee from Ohio, I shouldn't be so caught up with Robert E. Lee's family home," she said as they left Stratford Hall, "but the place is so beautiful and so fascinating. I wish I'd lived back then. Imagine having his family and the Washingtons for neighbors. Just think what the dinner conversations must have been like."

Richard grinned at her. "Not unlike the conversation at one of Destiny's dinner parties when she invites half of the power brokers in D.C. I'll have to make sure you're at the next one. Destiny likes to throw off a controversial spark and see what it ignites."

"Yes, I imagine that would delight her. She told me about the incredibly lively and intellectual gatherings she used to have in her studio in France."

Richard regarded her with surprise. "She did? She never talks about France with us."

"Really?" Melanie's expression turned thoughtful. "Maybe she doesn't want to sound as if she misses it."

"Why on earth would she be afraid to let us see that she had a life before she came home to us?" he asked, then sighed as the answer came to him. "Because she doesn't want us to think for a second that she made a sacrifice."

"I suspect that's it," Melanie said. "Maybe you should ask her about it sometime."

"I probably should," he admitted. "I wonder if she and Ben ever talk about it. That's when she was painting. It's what they have in common. They both love art. She nurtured his talent unselfishly, but I sometimes wondered if she missed painting herself.'' He felt oddly left out to think that there was a part of Destiny she had kept from him, a part she might have shared with at least one of his brothers, a part she had definitely shared with Melanie, a comparative stranger at the time.

Melanie seemed to guess the direction of his thoughts. ''If she kept silent, it was because she didn't think you were ready to hear about the life she had in France, not because she loved you less.''

''I know that,'' he snapped impatiently.

''Do you really?'' Melanie asked quietly. ''I think what she did was one of the most unselfish acts I've ever heard about. She had a wonderful life, Richard. She was living a charmed life in a place she loved. She was madly in love. Her paintings were selling in Paris and along the French Riviera. She had friends. She was even a bit famous in her world. But when you, Mack and Ben needed her, she never gave any of it a second thought. She was here for you. For her, family came first. That's the only thing that really matters.''

It was true. Richard had always known that his aunt had made sacrifices for them, but he'd never guessed how many. Or maybe as a child he hadn't wanted to know. And as an adult, her presence was a given, something he no longer questioned. How astonishing that it had taken Melanie to make him see a whole other side to Destiny. For the first time he was seeing her as a remarkable woman, not just as his aunt.

''You're amazing,'' he said, pressing a kiss to Melanie's cheek, grateful to her for making him put Destiny's sacrifices into perspective.

"Thank you, but what did I do?"

"Opened my eyes." And his heart, he added silently.

The brief vacation from the world passed in a blissful haze. If it hadn't been for the one thing Richard hadn't said—that he loved her—Melanie would have been totally content and rapturously happy.

They stayed up late, watched movies and ate popcorn. They danced to oldies on the radio. They made love in front of the fire time and again. Each time was a revelation, showing her new insights into everything but his heart. She despaired of that ever changing.

On New Year's Eve at the stroke of midnight, she was cradled in his arms, spent but filled with contentment, when he gazed into her eyes, "There's something we need to discuss before we go home tomorrow," he said. "It's a new year, time for new beginnings."

There was hope to be found in his words, but his tone filled Melanie with a sense of dread. "What?"

He looked away from her. "The very public breakup I promised you."

"You've been thinking about that?" she asked dully. She'd dared to envision happily-ever-after, and he'd been focused on extricating himself from the lie, starting the new year fresh without her and all of the complications she represented.

"Haven't you?" he asked. "You said all along it was something we should do sooner rather than later. I think you were right. After what happened with Destiny the other day, all the shopping and planning, we can't let this continue."

"This is it, then," she said bravely, refusing to

allow one single traitorous tear to fall. "What do you have in mind?"

He met her gaze then, searching her face for something, but she was determined not to let him see the hurt ripping her apart. Instead, she fought to keep her gaze neutral.

"I thought you should decide," he said, his voice suddenly flat and emotionless.

Melanie nodded, because she didn't trust herself to speak.

"You'll think about it?" he prodded. "You'll let me know? I'll go along with whatever you want."

"Do you want to do this very soon?" she asked when she could keep her voice steady.

"I think that's best," he said, his gaze averted.

"So do I," she said. Then she could get on with the business of mending her broken heart.

Suddenly chilled to the bone, she reached for the chenille throw on the sofa, stood up and wrapped herself in it. "I'm going to bed," she said in a voice so choked she barely recognized it as her own.

Richard didn't reach for her, said nothing to stop her. Only when she was at the foot of the stairs did he call out softly.

"Happy new year, Melanie."

"Happy new year," she replied automatically, but her heart wasn't in it. If anything, this new year was off to the worst start ever.

Upstairs, she barely resisted the desire to throw things. Unless something hit Richard in the head and knocked some sense into him, what would be the point?

Couldn't he see what she saw? They could be happy together. She knew it. She could help him get wherever he wanted to go in life. She'd be the perfect match for a man who needed some balance for all the demands he put on himself. She'd keep him from being stodgy.

But her hope of any future had died the instant he'd brought up the great breakup scene. Despite the emotional and physical connection she'd experienced over the past few days, they were obviously in very different places. To him this had apparently been nothing more than an interlude, something inevitable that had been building between them, something neither of them could have ignored forever. It hadn't meant anything, at least not to Richard.

Melanie knew better than most that it was impossible to make someone fall in love. It was equally impossible to make them admit to love when they were too afraid to recognize the emotion. When it came to that, she was as cowardly as Richard.

So to protect her stupid pride and her heart, she would go back to Alexandria and throw herself into planning the party at which she would throw that damnable ring back in his face. She would make the scene so believable, so memorable, that it would haunt him forever. Richard might be willing to toss away what they'd had, but he'd never forget her.

Sadly, she wasn't likely to forget him, either.

Chapter Fifteen

Melanie hated the fact that she was deliberately going to ruin Destiny's engagement party for them by creating a scene, but Richard's aunt had virtually given her no choice. With her usual impulsiveness, Destiny had already been well into planning the event when Richard and Melanie returned from their getaway. With invitations already at the printer's, it had been too late to turn back.

Since Melanie and Richard had concluded it was best to end the charade before it went on too much longer, the party was the most public way of accomplishing that. This way everyone would find out at once that she and Richard were no longer together. She'd even invited Pete Forsythe so he could witness the end of the romance his sleazy reporting—albeit at Destiny's instigation—had triggered in the first place.

"Are you absolutely certain you don't want your

parents to fly over for the party?'' Destiny asked as they were doing one final check of the guest list. ''I'm sure Richard would be happy to send the company jet for them.''

And have them here for this debacle? No way, Melanie thought. It was bad enough that they were likely to read about it in some wire service tidbit in their morning paper.

She had, however, insisted on having Becky at the party. She was going to need at least one friendly face in the crowd when things blew up.

''My parents hate flying,'' she told Destiny truthfully. It was just about the only honest thing to cross her lips lately. ''And Dad can't get off work in the middle of the week to drive over. I'm sure they'll want to throw their own party in Ohio sometime down the road.''

Probably when she was forced to move back home because her career here had gone up in flames, she thought despondently.

''Melanie, is everything all right?'' Destiny asked, regarding her worriedly. ''For a bride-to-be, you don't seem very happy. You've looked sad ever since you and Richard got back from your little romantic getaway.''

''I'm just tired,'' she assured Destiny. ''We did too much and my desk was piled high when I got back, so I've been working a lot of late hours.''

Destiny seemed to accept the explanation. ''Once you and Richard are married, you could stop working,'' she said carefully. ''I know that's not a very modern attitude, but you certainly could afford to quit.''

"I love what I do," Melanie told her. And soon it was going to be the most important thing in her life.

"I know and you're good at it, but sometimes life forces us to prioritize. At some point your family might need to come first."

"The way it did for you?"

Destiny's expression remained neutral. "Yes," she said quietly. "The way it did for me."

"Have you ever regretted it?"

Destiny looked shocked. "How could I? Richard, Mack and Ben are like sons to me. They needed me," she said fiercely. "I could never have lived with any other choice."

Melanie heard the total conviction in her voice, even though she also thought she heard a faint note of wistfulness, something Destiny would never voice aloud. If there were regrets, she would clearly take them to her grave. It was not a burden she would place on her nephews.

"How do you know when the choice is right?" Melanie asked, her own wistfulness far more evident.

Destiny smiled at her. "You ask your heart. It will never lie to you, not about anything important." Then she added wryly, "Of course, sometimes you have to listen carefully to hear it through all the clatter going on around you."

Melanie wondered about that. Her heart seemed to have quite a track record of getting it wrong. Before she could pursue that thought, Richard came into the very feminine office that Destiny maintained at Carlton Industries. It was a stark contrast to the clean, modern lines in the other offices.

He came over and gave Destiny an absentminded peck on the cheek, then dropped an equally impersonal kiss on Melanie's lips to maintain the charade for the moment. Even knowing it meant nothing, Melanie still felt the touch curl her toes.

"What are you two up to?" he asked.

"Finalizing plans for the engagement party," Destiny said. "The invitations are going out this afternoon."

He met Melanie's gaze, his expression guarded. "Has Destiny roped you into inviting a cast of thousands?"

"Only hundreds," Melanie said. "I cut her off when we hit three hundred and fifty."

"A nice round number," he said wryly. "Any media?"

"Pete Forsythe," Melanie told him. "And his photographer."

Destiny shook her head. "Why you want to invite Forsythe is beyond me."

Richard regarded her with amusement. "I thought you were rather fond of Mr. Forsythe."

Destiny looked suitably appalled. Melanie was impressed by her ability to feign indignation.

"Why would you think such a thing?" Destiny inquired coolly.

"You did use him to get that item about my cozy little getaway with Melanie in the paper a few weeks back," he reminded her. "Why not give him the inside scoop on the resulting engagement?"

"Whatever," Destiny said airily.

"Indeed," Richard replied. Then he asked, "Mind if I steal Melanie away? We need to firm up some plans of our own."

"By all means," Destiny said eagerly.

Melanie reluctantly followed Richard back to his office. "Is this about the campaign?"

He shook his head. "You quit, remember?"

"That doesn't mean you can't ask me something in an unofficial capacity," she told him, regretting now that all their ties were about to be severed.

"Well, it's not about the campaign. I needed to ask you about something else. I have a business dinner to attend tonight. Will you come along?"

Melanie stared at him. "Under the circumstances, don't you think that's a bad idea?"

"Probably, but these people will be offended if you're not there. They've heard about you, and they're anxious to meet you before the big party."

Melanie hated this. How could she go out with Richard tonight and fake being deliriously happy in front of strangers when she was already plotting their breakup?

"Could we have a spat tonight and end things before dinner?" she inquired hopefully. "Then we wouldn't have to go through with the rest of this, not dinner tonight, not the party, none of it."

He regarded her curiously. "I thought you wanted the big scene. It was one of the conditions when we went into this phony engagement."

"Honestly, I'm losing my taste for it." She didn't want to humiliate him, any more than she was looking forward to embarrassing herself or spoiling Destiny's hope for the two of them. She just wanted it all over with.

She reached for her ring and tried to twist it off. "Let's end this quietly, here and now."

Unfortunately, the ring wasn't budging. Nor, judging from the grim scowl on Richard's face, was he.

"You picked the time and place," he reminded her. "Backing out now is out of the question."

"Why?"

"It just is," he said, his expression set stubbornly.

If she hadn't known better, she might have entertained the crazy thought that he was trying to buy himself a little more time. But of course that couldn't be.

He should have let Melanie have her way and ended things in his office the other day when she'd pleaded with him to get it over with, Richard thought as he forced himself to take out his tuxedo in preparation for the upcoming engagement party.

What idiotic part of his brain had thought that waiting another week was a good idea? If he'd been hoping that having dinner with a couple of business associates would change anything, he'd been sadly mistaken. That evening, much like this one was destined to be, had been a disaster. Melanie had been quiet and withdrawn. The other couples had been uncomfortable. He wouldn't be a bit surprised if the deal they'd been discussing fell apart. Not that he could manage to work up much dismay over that. All of his dismay seemed to be reserved for the prospect of losing the only women he'd ever allowed himself to love.

"Why so glum?" Mack asked, when he found Richard pouring himself a stiff drink. "Tonight's party is supposed to be a celebration."

"Oh, can it," Richard retorted. "We both know better than that."

Mack seemed genuinely surprised by his reminder. "But I thought—"

"What? That something had changed? That we really were going to go through with the engagement and the wedding?"

"Yes, as a matter of fact," Mack said. "All the signs were pointing in that direction, especially when the two of you slipped out of town for a romantic little getaway."

"Well, where Melanie and I are concerned, things often aren't what they seem to be. She chose that time to let me know that we were going through with the previous arrangement."

Mack gave him a hard look. "And you did what to persuade her not to?"

"What was I supposed to do?" Richard demanded. "She'd obviously made up her mind."

Mack groaned. "Did you tell her you loved her?"

Richard frowned at him.

"I'll take that as a no," Mack concluded. "What is wrong with you? Never mind. I know the answer to that. Believe me, I'm as gun-shy when it comes to romance as you are, but we're talking Melanie here, bro. The woman is crazy in love with you, and you're obviously in love with her. Don't let her slip through your fingers."

Richard wasn't ready to admit his feelings, not even to a man he trusted with his life. "You're forgetting one thing. This whole engagement thing has been a farce to prove something to Destiny."

Mack, damn him, laughed. "You still think Destiny doesn't know that? You're delusional. All of this may have started as a stupid, immature game—"

Richard's scowl deepened.

"Don't pull that look on me, big brother," Mack said, undaunted. "You can't intimidate me. The important thing here is to admit that the game is over and try to fix everything before it's too late. Don't be stubborn, Richard. Not about something this important. If you want to make the whole engagement thing real, it's entirely possible that she does, too, but was too scared to admit it given your ridiculous agreement about an exit strategy.''

Richard stared at him, startled by Mack's insight. Could it be that Mack was right? Had he simply backed Melanie into a corner, the same way she'd backed him into one, both of them unwilling to risk being vulnerable?

''When did you get to be so smart, especially about matters of the heart, Mack?''

''I'm not the stupid one, bro. You're the one who hasn't seen the handwriting on the wall till now.''

It seemed pointless to keep denying his feelings when Mack wasn't buying it. ''Then what do I do?''

''You'll think of something, some grandstand play, and don't take no for an answer. Melanie can stage her scene, then you stage yours. I'll put my money on you.''

With that kind of faith in his persuasiveness, how could Richard say no? Not when it meant getting the only thing he'd ever wanted this desperately. He picked up the phone and called his jeweler, then gazed at his brother.

''I have an idea, it just might work.''

''Even if it doesn't, at least you'll know that you did everything you could. That's a hell of a lot better than giving up without a fight.''

Mack was right, Richard concluded, feeling marginally better. He knew all about the importance of seizing the initiative in a negotiation. Why the hell had the tactic slipped his mind until now, when this was the most important deal he was ever likely to close?

Melanie was impatiently swiping at tears when Destiny found her in the ladies' room moments before she was supposed to break her engagement. Until now the party had been a rousing success. She should have been smiling. In fact, she had been smiling till her jaw ached. She'd come in here when she couldn't bear it a moment longer.

"Darling, is anything wrong?" Destiny asked, her expression oddly smug rather than worried or sympathetic.

Melanie studied Destiny's expression, then sighed. Mack had been right. Destiny knew exactly what she and Richard had been up to. "You've known all along, haven't you? You've known that it was a charade?"

"Of course I have," Destiny said cheerfully, as if she hadn't just blown a fortune to celebrate something that had never been. She patted Melanie's hand. "But I also know you're in love with my nephew and he's in love with you. I don't have a doubt in my mind about that."

Melanie didn't ask her how she knew that. She needed advice and she needed it in a hurry. "Then how do I fix this?"

"You don't," Destiny advised gently. "You let Richard fix it. There are some things men have to figure out for themselves. Otherwise the balance of power is always off."

"Do you think he will?" Melanie asked plaintively.

"If he's even half the man I think he is, you'll be walking down the aisle in a month," Destiny declared confidently. "And no one knows my nephew better than I do."

"Then I break up with him as planned?"

Destiny nodded. "He'll be expecting it. Don't disappoint him. Or if he's been counting on a last-minute change of heart, this will really shake him up."

An hour later Melanie took a deep breath and tossed a glass of champagne in Richard's face. It wasn't what she'd mentally scripted for the opening gambit in the scene, but it felt good. Sometimes the man was so dense, she could barely stand it. Maybe the champagne would snap him to his senses.

"What the hell was that for?" he demanded, looking genuinely shocked.

"I was hoping it would wash some of that fog away from your eyes so you'd start seeing things more clearly."

Suddenly, to her surprise, he chuckled. "Is that so?"

"Yes, it's so. For a supposedly smart man, you're dumber than dirt about some things." Okay, this wasn't the way Destiny had advised her to go, but Melanie was tired of leaving her fate in other people's hands. She'd left it to Destiny, Richard, the gods, for too long already. She'd forgotten that she was in charge of her own future, that no one cared more about the outcome of this relationship more than she did...unless it was Richard.

"Are you breaking up with me?" he inquired, clearly amused despite the large sea of stunned faces surrounding them.

"Yes," she said very firmly.

"Do I get the ring back?"

She held out her hand and considered the huge rock that she'd hated from the beginning. It sparkled brilliantly in the lights from the ballroom's fancy chandeliers. The stupid thing must be six carats, with perfect clarity and color. It was worth a fortune. "I don't think so. I think I'll pawn it to help me expand my company."

Behind her, she heard his brothers chuckle.

Richard shrugged, not nearly as outraged by that as she'd expected.

"Okay, then," he said mildly, "but I think you're going to want to take it off now."

Melanie faced him stubbornly. "Why would I do that?"

He pulled a velvet jeweler's box from his pocket. "I've got another one I think maybe you'll like better."

Melanie felt her mouth gape. "You're proposing to me? Here? Now? For real?"

She heard a delighted gasp behind her and whirled on Destiny. "Oh, put a sock in it. This is exactly what you were counting on from the beginning. You said you knew him better than anyone."

Destiny's eyes were filled with laughter. "Trust me, darling, I didn't know about this."

Richard grinned. "You should have guessed. You did put it all into motion, didn't you?"

"I can't take all the credit," she said with surprising modesty.

Richard didn't seem impressed by her sudden sense of humility. "You should know by now that Destiny always gets what she wants," he confided to Melanie.

Destiny beamed at Richard and Melanie, then

turned to his brothers, a sparkle of pure mischief in her eyes. "Something you two need to remember, too."

Mack and Ben, their expressions instantly horrified, suddenly melted into the crowd. Watching them disappear, Melanie turned to Richard. "When their turns come, whose side are you going to be on?"

"Destiny's, of course," he said without hesitation. "She's made me a believer in the power of love." He looked deep into Melanie's eyes. "You still haven't given me an answer, by the way."

Melanie smiled. "I should make you wait, maybe torment you a little."

She heard Destiny mutter something about the balance of power again and made up her mind. She knew what it had cost Richard to put his heart on the line in this room filled with people. He'd taken the risk. The least she could do was reciprocate here and now.

"I accept," she told him, her gaze locked with his.

Their obviously baffled guests, who'd come to celebrate an engagement, seen it broken, then back on again, cheered wildly, taking their cue from Destiny, who swept Melanie into a hug and congratulated her.

"I couldn't have asked for a better woman for Richard," she said.

Melanie chuckled. "You act surprised. We both know you handpicked me, though I've yet to figure out why."

"Oh, darling, that one's easy," Destiny said, turning her to face Richard, who was more at ease than Melanie had ever seen him. His eyes filled with emotion when he caught her looking his way.

"Can you see what I see?" Destiny asked.

"He's happy," Melanie realized, recognizing the signs because she was filled with jubilation herself.

"He's happy," Destiny confirmed. "Because of you."

Melanie gave her a fierce hug. "Maybe we should share the credit."

Destiny nodded, her expression smug. "Yes, perhaps we should for tonight, but I think over time the lion's share will go to you. I'll thank you in advance for that."

Melanie's gaze lingered on Richard. "He's able to love me at all because of you," she told Destiny honestly. "Your work here is done."

"Yes, I believe it is." She looked around the room. "Now where the dickens do you suppose Mack is?"

Melanie chuckled at Destiny's eagerness as she began moving through the crowd in search of Mack. "You probably ought to find your brother and warn him," she told Richard when he joined her.

"Hell no," Richard said. "Mack can take care of himself. In fact, it'll be a pleasure to watch him squirm for a change. Besides, I have more important things to do."

"Oh? Such as?"

"This," he said, lowering his head to capture her mouth.

"Definitely more important," Melanie murmured against his lips.

"Have I mentioned that I love you?" Richard asked when the kiss ended.

"Come to think of it, no," Melanie said. "But I thought it was implicit in your proposal."

He smiled. "I knew you could read my mind."

She sighed. "There was a while there when I was

sure I'd gotten it all wrong. From now on, though, I think I'll trust my instincts.''

''What are your instincts telling you now?'' he asked.

She studied him thoughtfully, then grinned. ''Shame on you,'' she scolded.

''Then you're not interested in blowing off this party and getting a room upstairs?''

''I didn't say I wasn't interested,'' she replied. ''I can see you're going to have to work on reading my mind.''

His expression sobered. ''I'll make it my life's mission. That and loving you.''

Melanie felt her heart swell. If he said it, she could bank on it. Richard Carlton always kept his promises. That was the backbone of his campaign strategy and, best of all, it was the truth.

* * * * *

And now, turn the page for a sneak preview of PRICELESS, *the second book in Sherryl Woods's exciting new miniseries,* MILLION-DOLLAR DESTINIES.

On sale April 2004 from Silhouette Special Edition.

Chapter One

"If Mack Carlton had a life, if he had a family, if he had *anything* important to do, he wouldn't be wasting his money on a football team."

Rather than the indignant protests she'd expected, Beth was stunned when every man around her in the hospital cafeteria fell silent. Guilty looks were exchanged, the kind that said humiliation was just around the corner.

"You sure you don't want to reconsider that remark?" Jason asked, giving her an odd, almost pleading look.

"Why would I want to do that?"

"Because I'm pretty sure you mentioned when we started this discussion that you've been trying to get Mack Carlton in here to visit with Tony Vitale," Jason said. "The kid's crazy about him. You thought meeting Mack might lift his spirits since the chemo hasn't been going that well."

Her gaze narrowed. "So? This community-minded paragon of football virtue hasn't bothered to respond to even one of my calls."

Jason cleared his throat and gestured behind her.

Oh, hell, she thought as she slowly turned and stared up at the tall, broad-shouldered man in the custom-tailored suit who was regarding her with a solemn, steady gaze. He had a faint scar under one eye, but that did nothing to mar his good looks. In fact, it merely added character to a perfectly sculpted face and drew attention to eyes so dark, so enigmatic, that she trembled under the impact. Everything about his appearance spoke of money, taste and arrogance, except maybe the hairstyle, which had a Harrison Ford style of spikiness to it.

"Dr. Browning?" he inquired in an incredulous tone that suggested he'd been expecting someone older and definitely someone male.

Despite the unspoken but definitely implied insult, his quiet, smooth voice eased through Beth, then delivered a belated punch. She tried to gather her wits and to form the apology he deserved, but the words wouldn't come. She'd never have deliberately insulted him to his face, even if she did have an abundance of scorn for men who wasted money on athletic pursuits that could be better spent on saving mankind.

"She'll be with you as soon as she gets her foot out of her mouth," Jason said, breaking the tension.

Grateful to the radiologist for helping her out, she managed to stand and offer her hand. "Mr. Carlton, I wasn't expecting you."

"Obviously," he said, his lips curving into a slow

smile. "My aunt said you'd had trouble contacting me. My staff shouldn't have put you off. I apologize for that."

Beth had read that he was a heartbreaker. Now she knew why. If his gaze could render her speechless, that smile could set her on fire. Add in the unexpected touch of humility and the sincerity of his apology, and her first impression was pretty much smashed to bits. She'd never experienced a reaction to any man quite like this. She wasn't sure she liked it.

"Would you…?" Exasperated by her inability to gather her thoughts, she swallowed hard, took a deep breath, then tried again. "Would you like a cup of coffee?"

"Actually I'm on a tight schedule. I found myself near here and wanted to let you know that I haven't been deliberately blowing off your calls. I thought I'd take a chance that now would be a good time to meet Tony."

"Of course," she said at once, knowing what such a visit would mean even if regular visiting hours were later in the day. This was one instance when she didn't mind breaking the rules. "I'll take you to his room. He'll be thrilled."

Jason cleared his throat. At his pointed look, Beth realized that her colleagues were hoping for an introduction to the local football legend. Amazed that grown men could be as enamored of Mack Carlton as her twelve-year-old patient was, she paused and made the introductions.

When it seemed that the doctors were about to go over every great play the man had ever made on the football field, she cut them off.

"As much as you guys would probably like to discuss football for the rest of the day, Mr. Carlton is here to see Tony,'' she reminded them a bit curtly.

Mack Carlton gave her another of those smiles that could melt the polar ice cap. ''Besides,'' he said, ''we're probably boring Dr. Browning to tears.''

Now there was a loaded statement if ever she'd heard one. She didn't dare admit to being bored and risk insulting him more than she had when he'd first arrived and overheard her. Nor was she inclined to lie. Instead she forced a smile. ''You did say you had a tight schedule.''

His grin spread. ''So I did. Lead the way, Doctor.''

Relieved to have something concrete to do, she set off briskly through the corridors to the unit where twelve-year-old Tony had spent far too much of his young life.

''Tell me about Tony,'' Mack suggested as they walked.

''He's twelve and he has leukemia,'' Beth told him, fighting to keep any trace of emotion from her voice. It was the kind of story she hated to tell, especially when the battle wasn't being won. ''It's the third time it's come back. This time he's not responding so well to the chemotherapy. We'd hoped to get him ready for a bone-marrow transplant, but we don't have the right donor marrow, and because of his difficulty with the chemo, I'm not so sure it would be feasible for him right now anyway.''

Mack listened intently to everything she was saying. ''His prognosis?''

''Not good,'' she said tersely.

''And you're taking it personally,'' he said quietly.

Beth promptly shook her head. ''I know I can't win every battle,'' she said, as she had to the psychologist who'd expressed his concern about her state of mind earlier in the day. Few people knew just how personally she took a case like Tony's. She was surprised that Mack Carlton had guessed it so easily.

"But you hate losing," Mack said.

"When it's a matter of life and death, of course I do," she said fiercely. "I went into medicine to save lives."

"Why?" Before she could reply, he added, "I know it's a noble profession, but dealing with sick kids has to be an emotional killer. Why you? Why this field?"

She was surprised that he actually seemed interested in her response. "I was drawn to it early on," she said, aware that she was being evasive by suggesting that it hadn't been the motivating force in her entire life. With any luck, Mack wouldn't realize it.

"Because?" he prodded, not accepting the response at face value and proving once more that he was a more insightful man than she'd expected him to be.

"Why does it matter to you?" she asked, still dodging a direct answer to his question.

His eyes studied her intently. "Because it obviously matters to you."

Once again, his insight caught her off guard. It was evident he wasn't going to let this go until he'd heard at least some version of the truth. "Okay, here it is in a nutshell. I had an older brother who died of leukemia when I was ten," she told him, revealing more than she had to anyone else other than her family. They knew all too well what her motivation had been for choosing medicine, and they hadn't entirely approved of her choice, fearing she was doomed to repeated heartaches. "I vowed to save other kids like him."

Mack regarded her with what appeared to be real sympathy. "Like I said, you take it personally."

She sighed at the assessment. "Yes, I suppose I do."

"How long do you think you can keep it up, if you take every case to heart?"

"As long as I have to," she insisted tightly. "I only see a few patients. Most of my time is spent in research. Our treatments are getting better and better all the time." Sadly, Tony wasn't responding well to any of them, which was why she'd taken such an intense interest in his case.

"But not with Tony," Mack said.

Beth fought against the salty sting of unexpected tears. "Not with Tony, at least not yet," she admitted softly. Then she set her jaw and regarded Mack defiantly, blinking back those tell-tale tears. "But we're going to win this battle, too."

He gave her an admiring look. "Yes, I think you will," he said quietly. "Will my being here actually help Tony?"

"Hopefully it will improve his spirits," Beth assured him. "He's been a little down lately, and sometimes boosting a child's morale is the most important thing we can do. We need to keep him from giving up on himself or on us."

Mack nodded. "Okay, then. Let's go in there and talk football." He gave her an impudent grin. "I assume you won't be saying much."

Beth laughed despite herself, liking Mack far more than she'd ever expected to. She could forgive a lot in a person who had a sense of humor, whether about her foibles or his own. "Probably not."

His expression sobered. "Good. What I do for a living may not be medicine or rocket science, but I'd hate to have you dismiss it in front of a kid who thinks it matters."

Beth stared at him as his point struck home. Her opinion of football or of Mack Carlton didn't matter right now. "Touché, Mr. Carlton. I'll definitely refrain from comment. This is all about Tony."

He winked. "Call me Mack. My fans do."

"I'm not one of your fans."

"Stick around," he taunted lightly. "You might be after this."

Beth bit back a sigh. Yes, she could be, she admitted to herself. Not that Mighty Mack Carlton needed another conquest in his life. The gossip columns were littered with the names of women who thought they had the inside track in his life. She'd noticed that few of them ever got a second mention. She wasn't the least bit inclined to test her luck in an already crowded field.

"Don't hold your breath, Mr. Carlton. Besides, the only person whose adoration counts is Tony and you've already got a lock on that."

"I wouldn't mind at least a hint of approval from you, too," he said, his gaze capturing hers and holding it.

Despite the obvious attempt to disconcert her, Beth felt herself falling under his spell. She found it irritating. "Why? Do you have to win over every woman you meet?"

He hesitated then and an odd look that might have

been confusion flickered in his eyes. "How well do you know my aunt?" he asked.

The out-of-the-blue question caught her off guard. "Your aunt?"

"Destiny Carlton, the woman you contacted who made sure I came over here today."

Beth shook her head. "I don't believe we've met," she said. "Though I recognize the name. I think she raises a lot of money for the hospital. I never spoke to her, though."

Mack seemed surprised. "You really don't know her?"

"No."

"And you didn't call her?"

"No. Why?"

He shook his head, obviously more puzzled than ever. "Doesn't matter."

Despite his denial, Beth got the distinct impression that it mattered a lot. She simply had no idea why.

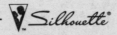

SPECIAL EDITION™

Susan Mallery

presents the continuation
of the bestselling series

**Watch how
passion flares
under the hot
desert sun for
these rogue sheiks!**

THE SHEIK &
THE PRINCESS IN WAITING
(Silhouette Special Edition #1606)

Prince Reyhan had been commanded by his father,
the king of Bahania, to marry as befit his position.
There was just one tiny matter in the way:
divorcing his estranged wife Emma Kennedy.
Seeing the lovely Emma again brought back
a powerful attraction…and a love long buried.
Could Reyhan choose duty over his heart's desire?

Available April 2004 at your favorite retail outlet.